DELICIOUS PAIN

PORTIA DA COSTA

Copyright © 2018 by Portia Da Costa

All rights reserved.

No part of this book may be reproduced in any form or by any electronic or mechanical means, including information storage and retrieval systems, without written permission from the author, except for the use of brief quotations in a book review.

❦ Created with Vellum

CONTENTS

FORBIDDEN TREASURES

Chapter 1	3
Chapter 2	12
Chapter 3	26
Chapter 4	35

IN SEBASTIAN'S HANDS

Introduction	41
Life, the Universe and Sebastian	43
It's Time	55
The Roses in Your Cheeks	69
An Appointment with Her Master	85
Naughty Thoughts	103
Thank You!	115
About Portia	117
Self-published Ebooks by Portia	119
Mainstream Erotic Romance by Portia	121
Another Appointment - Excerpt	123

FORBIDDEN TREASURES

ONE

"Now don't go crazy. Remember we're supposed to be economizing."

Alice Porter quivered. Why did it turn her on so when her husband pretended to be stern with her like this? Julian gave her a wink and a cool kiss on the cheek as they were about to part at the entrance to the flea market, and it was all she could do not to grab him and drag him back to the car to make out.

"I know, I know. I'll be careful." She grinned at him, defiant. He knew she was only paying lip service to his instructions, and the way his blue eyes narrowed made her heart leap and lust surge in her belly. This morning, in bed, he'd been ferocious. Deliciously loving, but all power, all command.

We should have stayed at home, in bed.

As Julian walked away, no doubt heading for the militaria and the vintage engineering items, she watched his fine ass and his long legs in narrow blue jeans recede into the distance, and she wished she were beneath him, between the sheets.

Trying to distract herself, Alice focused on the market. It was a fabulous one, the largest and the most tempting they'd visited in ages. Stall after stall was crammed with second hand clothes, crafts, records, and most of all bric-a-brac; a positive cornucopia of hand-me-down treasures, some genuinely antique and some quite modern.

She and Julian never wanted to look at the same things, so it was much better for mutual harmony if they split up and each explored and scrounged alone. He was a swift and decisive chooser; she liked to linger and ponder. It was no use sticking together and losing patience with one another.

After a few minutes wandering around, Alice discovered a treasure trove. What seemed to be the entire contents of a genuine Edwardian household, spread across several tables. For once, she found herself completely forgetting her lustful thoughts about her husband. There was so much in the hoard that she wanted to examine, and a lot she desperately wanted to buy. But Julian would go nuts if she splurged on everything she fancied. He wasn't miserly; he would probably come back laden with his own fair share of purchases. But he wasn't the wild spender that she was, not by a mile.

Deciding not to worry about her husband's possible reactions, Alice plunged in eagerly amongst the delightful vintage hoard.

The first things she happened upon as must-buys were a couple of pretty gilt picture frames, perfect for their old-fashioned kitchen dresser. There were still photographs in them, and they looked as bygone as the rest of items on display. Were they genuine Edwardian? It seemed so, judging by the clothes and the faded quality of the prints. One depicted a very proper looking gentleman, standing straight and four square, his eyes level and direct as he stared into the camera. He was holding a walking stick clutched firmly in his right hand.

Or is it a walking stick?

Alice peered more closely. No, perhaps it wasn't. The stick didn't look sturdy enough to bear much weight. In fact it look much too slim and whippy for that, more like a lightweight rattan cane, the sort used by an old-fashioned schoolmaster to dish out daily punishments in bygone and less enlightened times.

Crikey!

The idea of the Edwardian gentleman's cane being used for such a purpose made Alice's insides quiver again, the feeling much like the urges she'd felt when she'd been thinking about Julian making love to her, not ten minutes ago. Her face felt very hot all of a sudden, and in the pit of her belly a familiar ache gathered.

What on earth is the matter with me? Have I turned kinky?

In her mind, she pictured a pretty young woman, maybe someone much like herself, bent over and showing her bloomers to the stern gentleman in the photograph. Or perhaps showing him a good deal more than her bloomers? What would it be like to be that young woman, presenting her pale, bare bottom for chastisement with that cane? The image morphed again, and suddenly it was her husband she saw in dapper Edwardian dress; Julian swishing the cane as if it had been fashioned just for him.

"Good grief," murmured Alice, unsettled by the clarity of the mind-picture and the effect it had on her. Weird. Did she really want Julian to keep her in line that way? Would he even want to? He was a take-charge kind of man, but he was also tender and considerate, and he abhorred violence.

But still. This was different, and she knew that. Something about the eyes of the man in the photograph seemed to tell a hidden story, and it was a tale that was nothing to do with domestic discipline and everything to do with dark forbidden pleasure.

The matched photograph only seemed to confirm her suspicions. It showed a handsome and rather buxom young woman of about her own age, mid twenties or so, with a wickedly impish expression on her face. There was nothing cowed or fearful about her. The picture was old, but smiling woman almost twinkled with satisfaction.

Alice continued with her treasure hunt.

The next box revealed more goodies from the unknown bygone household. There was a small delicate china jug, presumably part of a tea set, and a large silver spoon that would be ideal for serving fruit or puddings. Alice added these to her hoard, and with them put a beautiful old book about the language of flowers.

The last receptacle she came to was a substantial iron-bound chest, an object both impressive and ugly at the same time somehow. It would look amazing in their hall, but Julian might draw the line at the price tag. Still, there might be something interesting inside it, so Alice unfastened its heavy clasp and heaved the lid up.

"Oh my God!"

Eyes wide, she grinned at the contents of the chest, and then reached for the picture of the Edwardian gentleman again.

It's the same one.

Almost in awe, Alice lifted out a slender, gleaming rattan cane. It was a little discolored in places, but still supple and disturbingly whippy. It was almost certainly the one in the photograph.

The mental images surged back into her mind.

She saw the voluptuous, smiling young woman lying face down across a bed, quite naked but for her shoes and stockings rolled down to her knees. The gentleman, presumably her husband, was plying the cane across her full and rounded bottom.

Oh Julian.

Running her fingers up and down the instrument, Alice shuddered, imagining what her own husband could do with it. What would it feel like to have this laid across her own buttocks, perhaps with some considerable force? Out of control, her mind leapt ahead. Wouldn't this be the perfect way for Julian to express his displeasure with her extravagance? She seemed to see the slim length of rattan balanced in his elegant fingers. She wouldn't transgress again in a hurry after making the acquaintance of this beauty, no doubt about that.

Don't be silly, Alice, you'd probably just transgress even sooner.

For a moment, the cane hovered over Alice's growing pile of purchases, but with some reluctance she laid it aside. There was a big difference between fantasy and reality. She reached into the chest again, and drew out another item that'd caught her eye. It was a small book, bound in gleaming, well cared for burgundy colored leather, possibly a ledger of some kind. Alice flipped it open.

The first page revealed its awesome purpose.

Written in a large, flowing hand, in black ink, were the words *Punishment Ledger* and beneath that was the legend: *Nathaniel Grayson, being the head of this household, and sworn to ensure its smooth running, and the chastisement of all those within it.*

The next page bore a name too—*Mrs. Prunella Grayson*

—and beneath that were a number of journal like entries, each ruled off, one after another.

The first read:

Today, my dear wife, Mrs. Grayson, did speak rather improperly while we were entertaining the Vicar's wife, causing that lady to go dead white with shock. In punishment, I required my dear wife to present herself at bedtime, appropriately prepared for a beating. This consisted of her placing herself over the end of the bed, raising her nightgown around her waist, and then waiting until I selected an appropriate implement; on this occasion, my leather carpet slipper. To the accompaniment of much crying and protesting, I administered thirty strokes of medium force, which rendered my dear wife's bottom a charming shade of flushed and regal pink, and her nature far more biddable, both in public and in our private dealings.

Alice glanced at the photo of Mrs. Grayson. There was nothing unhappy or penitent about her, nothing to suggest she resented her husband's stern treatment. In fact the very reverse was true. Mrs. Grayson looked a picture of contented fulfillment, and even allowing for the age of the photograph it was clear that her eyes were sparkling and merry.

She loves it, the sexy minx.

Alice turned the pages eagerly, and in the space of a few minutes she'd been drawn into the world of Mr. and Mrs. Grayson, and she longed to share it. Nostalgia overwhelmed her, a yearning for a time and a place and a society she had never experienced, but which she knew that she—and Julian—would relish.

She paused at the page for *Miss Sutherland, my son's governess* and read another long and detailed entry.

Today, I considered Miss Sutherland to be very lax in her

guidance of Geoffrey. He came in from the garden covered in mud, and later I found several of my prize petunia bushes to be somewhat battered, due to the playing of a boisterous game of cricket in their vicinity. The punishment of Geoffrey is in the hands of his governess, but it falls to me to remind that young lady of her responsibilities. To that effect, she reported to me in my office at five o'clock, and there I bade her bend over the back of a hard chair while I lifted her skirt and petticoat, and then slid down her drawers to her ankles. [I always feel a punishment to be most efficacious on a woman's naked posterior] She pleaded with me for clemency, and complained about the lack of dignity afforded her, but these remarks soon ceased as I laid about her exposed part with my belt. After a good twenty strokes, and many tears, Miss Sutherland proclaimed herself well reminded of her duties, and I feel she is right in this. For the next day or so at least, a sore and heated bottom should serve as an excellent 'aide memoire' both for her and for me. I shall have cause to reflect upon its condition from time to time with much satisfaction.

How many more women had fallen under Mr. Grayson's regime of dire chastisement? Alice flicked through the pages with scant respect for the ledger's great age. She wasn't in the least surprised to find several miscreants listed.

Mrs. Potter, the cook, spanked with her own wooden spoon for over-salting the soup, but noted as *a fine woman*, and *a true stoic, no tears* .

Not so Maisie, the parlor maid, who was reported as *bellowing like a heifer* when corrected with the back of a wooden clothes brush before an audience in the servants' hall. *It really serves little practical purpose to punish Maisie, as this is the fourth dish she has broken inside a fortnight. She should be dismissed, because she will never be a good or efficient servant, but her large, white rear makes such a satisfying target and the way she wriggles is most delightful.*

Alice smirked broadly; she couldn't help herself.

You only spanked them because you liked it, you dirty old goat.

Thumbing through the book, she devoured the outrageous entries. It wasn't until she heard a church clock chime that she realized how long she'd spent in the Grayson household. Time had flown by. With a pang of guilt for the total price she had to hand over to the stallholder, Alice gathered her purchases into a large carrier bag, and moved on.

Even if there had been more time to explore, the rest of the market seemed to have lost its charm now. There was no allure in old vinyl records, home made jam, and baskets of potpourri, no excitement in embroidery or second hand books. All she could think about was the Punishment Ledger in her carrier bag, and the trenchant cane she'd left behind her at the stall. She'd wanted it. Oh how she'd wanted it. But still, that atavistic twinge of apprehension at the time had made her leave it; her fear that sexy daydreams and hard rattan would turn out to be two very, very different things.

Yet still she regretted her lack of spirit, especially when she saw Julian's expression as he leant on the car, waiting for her. His handsome face was a picture of both amusement and feigned disapproval. He'd never looked sexier—or more dominant.

"What's all that?" he enquired as she set the carrier down on her lap.

"Just a few bits," Alice defended as he set the engine in gear and they pulled out of the car park.

He shook his blond head and his lips quirked in a familiar, despairing grin. "Oh, really?"

The journey home was spent in silence. Alice had expected a token lecture, just for form's sake, but instead Julian seemed to be as wrapped up in his thoughts as she was in hers of the ledger; his face was composed as he drove, almost on auto pilot, back to their house.

When the car slid to a halt, Alice was first into the house, eagerly unpacking her treasures, but making sure to tuck the ledger into a drawer in the sitting room that Julian never looked in. When he finally joined her in the room, her husband eyed her thoughtfully, as if he knew she was up to something, but he didn't challenge her. He didn't reveal the contents of his own large box of goodies either, just waggled his blond eyebrows when she murmured "Oh, really," back at him. Alice suspected it was yet more tomes, bound volumes of Second World War memoirs or some such, that they'd have to find room for on their bookshelves. Their evening passed as normal, companionable and easy, but Alice's skin seemed to prickle in a vaguely pleasant way all the time, as if electrified by her husband's probing gaze.

As bedtime approached, Alice crept into the sitting room to retrieve the ledger, while Julian was in his office studying his finds. She still wished she'd bought the cane too, although she'd no idea how she'd have finessed it past him, as it would have been too long to hide in the carrier bag. Despite the absence of the implement, she looked forward to hearing how Mrs. Grayson had fared under its reign. She'd no real idea what it might be like to live in a disciplinary household, but her instincts suggested that the cane would be the ultimate sanction, the *ne plus ultra* of chastisement devices. She couldn't begin to imagine what it felt like, but as she pushed open the sitting room, she tried.

"Oh, hell!"

TWO

Hovering on the threshold, she could only stare. There, in his favorite easy chair, sat Julian. His fair hair was wet from his shower and he wore only a pair of black denim jeans; both his feet and his smooth chest were bare. He was calm and composed, and seemed to be reading casually. What lay across his lap made Alice gasp.

It was the cane. The narrow discolored cane with its evocative curling handle and all the painful memories that were encoded along its shaft.

"This makes rather interesting reading, doesn't it?" said Julian in a slow, almost teasing tone as Alice hovered, nonplussed. He glanced up briefly, and then returned to his close study of the Punishment Ledger, his slender fingers caressing the cane as he did so.

"Y...yes." The words seemed to stick in Alice's throat. Her mind was a whirling torrent of possible futures. She walked slowly to where her husband sat, then halted before him.

"It seems that they had some pretty effective ways of dealing with domestic misbehavior back in the old days," he observed, his blue eyes dark, betraying humor and arousal, while his finely shaped mouth remained firm.

Although she didn't need Julian's permission to sit down, something in his manner made Alice remain on her feet. There was nothing at all about him that was like Mr. Grayson—the Edwardian disciplinarian was a stout and graying fellow with mutton chop whiskers, whereas Julian was slender, very blond and clean-shaven—but suddenly he had taken on the mantle of the keeper of the Ledger. He was so handsome that he always made her toes curl, but tonight he seemed darker somehow, delicious and very dangerous. He filled her with awe as he went on, his voice deceptively soft.

"Here's a good bit...'Today, my dear wife visited the milliner and did purchase four hats when I had expressly instructed her that one would suffice. Thus it has been my unfortunate task to administer the supreme sanction this evening. That is, my good and trusted cane, applied to her naked buttocks in six robust strokes. As ever, my darling did protest a very great deal, but with the assistance of Miss Sutherland, who held her down, I was able to complete the chastisement to my utmost satisfaction. So much so that, as I write this record, my dear one is lying face down on the bed beside me, with her delightful rear parts uncovered by either bed linen or night-gown. Though I do say it myself, the pattern of six crimson lines across her smooth white flesh is extraordinarily pleasing.'"

The slowly spoken and savored words still hung in the air as Julian closed the ledger with a muted snap that seemed to echo around the room, and then looked up, his blue eyes intent as he scrutinized Alice.

"He punished her for extravagance, Alice," he said, fingering the slender gleaming cane. "And I'll bet it was a lesson she didn't soon forget. I bet there wasn't a lot of overspending in that household for a while."

"No, I suppose not." Alice experienced a deep, melting feeling in her stomach, and an excitement lower down that made it hard for her to keep still. The urge to rub her thighs together, to ease the ache, was overpowering.

"Old fashioned methods have a lot to recommend them," her husband went on, still fondling the menacing length of rattan, "What do you think, sweetheart?" He twirled it now, deftly and cleverly, as if the damned thing had been designed for his fingertips.

"I think they probably worked... would work very well." Alice could hardly believe that she was speaking the words. She was effectively sealing her own fate at the hands of this exotic stranger who'd taken the place of her familiar beloved husband. This stern, breathtaking man, both forbidding and temporarily forbidden to her.

"In that case..." Julian nodded significantly, still twirling the cane.

Oh God, it's so hard! So thin! It'll really hurt!

Her eyes locked with Julian's, and they both looked down at the awesome object he was holding. It was such a plain thing yet latent with power.

"Oh no," he said, surprising her by setting the cane to one side, "I think we'll leave this little beauty for another time."

Julian shrugged, and Alice thought she saw a trace of trepidation. Was he unsure? Did he have just the same uncertainty and lack of experience that she did? For a moment, she wondered about her husband's past, and his secret urges that he'd never shared with her thus far. Had he done this before, played these games with a former lover?

Or was it *his* first time too? If it was, he was clearly a natural, and she trusted him despite her fluttering fear.

"I think we'll start off with something a little simpler, eh? Come over here," he said, patting his denim-clad knee.

Alice crept across to him, and then paused a foot away, unable to look him in the eye any more. He dazzled her, and at the same time, she felt a whole new persona settling over her too. She hung her head and studied her toes, feeling more penitent than she ever had in her life; a miscreant facing retribution in the full knowledge that she had been sinful enough to deserve it. She shook, and bit back a moan when she felt her husband's hands on the waistband of her jeans, unfastening the button, then whizzing down the zip.

"And I think we'll have a bit less of this sort of thing from now on." With a little shrug of disapproval, he tugged at the jeans, and then peeled them down her thighs. They fit her snugly, and they brought her skimpy knickers down with them, making her blush like fire. "I want to see you in pretty, feminine things a bit more often from now on. Skirts, slips, suspenders, nice, soft womanly knickers, lacy thongs. You should be able to afford plenty of new lingerie if you stop buying so much useless rubbish."

Without thinking, Alice clasped her hands over her pubic patch, but in a swift move, Julian snared her wrists and pulled her towards him. "Now, now, no need to be so modest," he said briskly, "You know I've seen all this plenty of times before. Let's have you across my knee, shall we?"

You have *done this before, haven't you?*

For a moment, Alice was distracted, unfocused. Who was the woman? Who had he punished?

Then Julian stroked the inside of her wrist with a fingertip, making everything right again, with a secret touch hidden in the game. He was with her now. He'd always be with her. This was what mattered, not the past.

Feeling as ungainly and gangling as a naughty, coltish girl, Alice did her best to obey him, almost tripping over the tangled clothing around her ankles. When she did get settled, she had the most precarious fear that she was going to topple head first off her husband's lap and onto the carpet. But instead, he held her firmly with a securing hand on her back, whilst presumably he studied the contours of her bottom.

"Ready then?" Both voice and fingertips were gentle as they cruised her bare skin. His exploration made her quiver again. "Do you understand why I have to do this?"

It was as if they were performing a ritual, each in their role, each serious, but also humming with desire. Alice nodded, and muttered a "yes", while her heart pounded and her mind filling with a very complex understanding indeed, a comprehension that went far beyond the simple shadow-play of punishment for misbehavior.

"Ouch!" she yelped as the first smack fell on her right buttock, and all her preconceptions about what it might have felt like came crashing down with Julian's hand.

Bloody hell, it hurts. It really hurts. I thought it was just going to feel like a gentle tap.

Moisture filled her eyes as a second, even crisper blow landed. Involuntarily, she groaned, squirming and shuffling on Julian's lap.

Dear God, how it smarted. How it stung. As more smacks descended in a fast and steady rhythm, it didn't take long before *all* of Alice's cheeks were flaming. Her dangling face was pink as a peony with a blend of embarrassment and excitement, and her bottom was so hot and throbbing that she was sure its entire surface was red and blotchy.

How have you learnt to do this? You must have picked it up somewhere. Don't tell me it's pure instinct. You know this.

The thoughts bobbed in her brain as her husband belabored her with skill and vigor. He was patterning the spanks around her cheeks, forming meticulous, overlapping circles and leaving no inch of flesh free of their fiery coverage. It was a master class and when her buttocks were pink and roasted, he tipped her body further forward and then aimed a volley of intensive wallops at the delicate under-hang; a zone so tender and thin-skinned that it made her squeal in a way that she would have found hilarious in some other circumstance.

"Now, now, my dearest," Julian said, his voice sounding like the very essence of Edwardian authority as he continued to spank and spank and spank, "Don't make such a fuss. This is *good* for you, you know." His hard hand struck her stunningly across her anus. "You've got to learn to like it." Two more slaps caught her thighs and made them sting. "Or how are you ever going to manage to take the cane?"

You tell me! Alice almost howled aloud as her bottom cheeks blazed with a life of their own. *I don't think I can take much more of this.*

As if he'd heard her, as if he'd read her mind with perfect clarity, Julian stopped far more suddenly than he'd begun. What Alice had expected to be another spank suddenly turned into a caress, even though with the state of her bottom it was like being stroked with a hand made of flame.

Julian smoothed the tips of his fingers over her bottom as if tracking the marks he'd made and the punishment he'd wrought. It taxed Alice more severely than the punishment itself had, and she squirmed and churned her hips, rubbing her crotch against his knee, massaging herself against denim clad muscle in an attempt to get relief.

She was more aroused than she'd ever been in her life, as well as being in the most complete discomfort she'd ever experienced too. Her sex throbbed and ached, the beat of it exactly matching the pounding ache in her hind parts.

"What do you want, Alice?"

Julian was leaning right over her now. She could feel his bare skin against her lower back and her arm. It was hot and silky and when she breathed in, he smelt wonderful, both fragrant with cologne and foxy with the sweat of his exertions.

She wanted him. In any way she could get him, the pain in her backside notwithstanding.

"Alice?" he prompted, and she realized she'd been drifting somewhere on a different plane of consciousness, buoyed up by pain endorphins and mind-bending sexual frustration.

"I...I want to come," she gasped, her voice sounding odd and hoarse, probably because she'd been shouting and squealing for about five minutes. Was it only that long? The spanks seemed to have been falling for a millennium.

"Come?" He said it low, and teasingly, like a caress in itself as his fingertips continued to torment her reddened bottom. He was dragging the very edge of his nails over her skin. Not heavily, in fact the action was almost feather-light, but it tasked her. It tasked her very hard. Every slow, taunting glide fueled her hunger.

Hampered by her jeans and knickers, she tried to part her thighs a bit more and rock herself against him. Julian pressed down firmly on the small of her back, steadying her. "Now, let's have the proper terminology, shall we? It's no casual matter," he murmured.

Alice groaned, her brain barely functioning as he drew a forefinger right up the crease of her bottom and circled her anus. She had trouble framing words, and she sifted frantically through the English language for something that might make even the slightest bit of sense. Eventually, while he was still lightly playing with her vent, she managed to speak.

"I want to have an orgasm."

"You want me to *give* you an orgasm, you mean? I haven't given you permission to have one on your own." His fingers moved on, exploring the juncture of buttock and thigh, investigating a particularly tender zone. "And you won't get anything at all until I hear you ask correctly."

"Please will you give me an orgasm."

She almost said *sir* or *master*, but she was still Alice, and her own woman, despite the fact that she adored him, and what he could do for her.

His fingers stilled and he gave a soft, merry little laugh. Leaning over more closely, he kissed her, his lips like a blessing on the side of her blushing face.

"Darling," he sighed, just a breath, then she felt him straighten up again, somehow both literally and figuratively, all business and dominion once again.

"You'll have to sit on my lap for an orgasm, and that's going to hurt. Can you bear up for that?" He trilled his fingers over the crown of her buttock, as if playing a flute.

"Yes. Yes, I can," said Alice through gritted teeth.

"Up you get then." He withdrew his hand from her bottom, and as Alice hauled herself to her feet, hiding her winces, he supported her.

I feel such a fool, standing here with my knickers and jeans round my ankles and my bottom bright red.

True, but somehow she was filled with pride too. She'd

endured. She'd met his challenge. She might look ludicrous to someone outside their circle of two, but daring to look into Julian's lambent eyes she saw only desire and respect, and his love, unmistakable. Glowing with something other than her spanked bottom, she stood as straight as she could, confident and flaunting. She even tilted her hips a little, teasing him with the promise of her sex.

Julian laughed softly and shook his head, making his blond curls glint in the lamplight. "You're incorrigible." Taking her hand he drew her down onto his lap again, making her sit this time.

Alice bit her lip. The denim of her husband's jeans was rough against her punished skin, stirring her spanked flesh anew. Yet still she shuffled, edging her tenderized thigh up close against his erection. He was huge and very hard, and despite his masterful act, he gave a little moan himself when she jostled herself against his arousal.

"Uh oh, what do you think you're doing, Alice?" he warned, but there was a smile in his voice, and his mouth was soft and accepting when she leaned in for a kiss.

For just a second or two, his lips yielded to her, and the sensation was as thrilling as it was confusing, their roles tilting like a seesaw. Then the world seemed to right itself again, and Julian slung one arm around her waist, and, with the other, cradled her jaw. His tongue plunged into her mouth and all was level again. With him in charge.

He kissed her hard and long, mastering her with his mouth and tongue as much as he'd done with his hand, the action as erotic as the spanking had been, if not more so. Waves of lasciviousness surged through Alice, a tide of lewdness. Despite the pain in her bottom, she writhed through the kiss, pressing her parted thighs down against his lap, knowing she was wetting the denim beneath her with her dew. She'd been holding onto him hard with both arms, but even as they kissed, she released with one, and tugged at the buttons of her cotton cardigan, opening it down the front. Her breasts were smallish and firm, and her bra was flimsy. She pushed and tugged it down to reveal herself to him, offering him the sight and the naked feel of her hardened nipples.

"Very nice. Very nice indeed," he whispered against her mouth, in between thrusts with is tongue, "I wonder if Mrs. Grayson was as naughty as you are. I'd like to think she sat on her hubby's lap afterwards so he could comfort her in the customary fashion."

"Oh, I'm sure she did," gasped Alice, her breath catching as Julian rolled one of her teats between his finger and thumb. The rough little action made her wriggle harder, and that made her bottom ache and burn. Between her legs, her core ached, calling for contact.

"Ask. Ask for what you want," Julian growled as if he'd read her mind again. Or perhaps he'd simply read her body.

"Please... Please Julian will you stroke me and make me have an orgasm."

His answer was one firm pinch to her nipple, which made her squeal, and then his hand sped swiftly to her sex, cupping it possessively. He didn't dive straight in, but just squeezed her pubis in a slow relentless rhythm.

Oh please.

The plea was silent this time, but Julian still heard her. Working with his long, nimble middle finger, he parted her thatch and slid through the curls, finding her center.

"Oh God...oh yes."

Aware that she was babbling clichés, Alice laughed aloud as she came, almost immediately and very hard. Her hips jerked, lurching up as if spring-loaded, jamming herself against Julian's hand as waves of pleasure beat and crashed through her body. In violent motion, she barely felt her soreness. It was there, but wasn't pain any more, as she understood it. All sensation served the ecstasy of orgasm.

Still chanting nonsense, she clamped her arms around her husband's neck, kissing more yeses and oh Gods against the side of his face, his ear and his soft, clean hair. She wasn't sure how long the climax lasted. It could've been seconds, but it felt like hours of bliss.

Eventually, and inevitably, it ebbed, but not with a sense of letdown, or post coital *tristesse*. Alice floated back to reality with a smile on her face, a sense of peace and joy, and deepest love—even though her well-spanked bottom still throbbed. Her death-grip on Julian's neck relaxed as she did, and she laughed again when he drew in a huge breath as if she'd been throttling him.

"I should spank you again for nearly choking the life out of me." His voice was soft and amused as he kissed her lightly on the corner of her mouth, then stroked her hair out of her eyes. It was damp where she'd been sweating.

"I'm going to need another shower now. That was...well, pretty much indescribable." Even to her own ears her voice sounded strange and breathy, as if she'd just traveled through a whirlwind.

"Me too." Julian took her hand, and conducted it authoritatively towards his groin. "But maybe you could oblige me first, if you don't mind?"

"Oh crikey, yes. Oh, I'm sorry." Alice giggled, feeling a sort of mad, gleeful hysteria bubble up. She'd almost forgotten about Julian's raging hard-on.

"Don't be. I've enjoyed myself. It's been a while." His hand closed hard around hers, massaging. "But I could really do with the *coup de grace* now, love, whenever you're ready."

It's been a while.

Alice didn't stop laughing, but she did start wondering. It didn't surprise her at all that her husband was experienced in spanking. It'd been patently obvious that he knew precisely what he was doing. What did surprise her was that she didn't mind. She waited a second for jealousy to kick in, but it didn't. Her over-riding emotion was intense curiosity.

"I'll tell you afterwards, Ali. We'll share a glass of wine and I'll tell you everything," said Julian, his voice tight. It was his turn to have hips that lifted and hitched about now. Alice smiled in amazement at the way he'd seemed to read her thoughts. He'd always been good at that, but now the gift seemed uncannier than ever.

"I'll keep you to that," said Alice sliding off his knee. She felt twinges of soreness in her bottom as she moved, but unless she was imagining things, they weren't quite as severe as they'd been before her orgasm. Had it acted as a kind of therapy, the release? She smiled to herself, gazing down at the vista of Julian's groin and the hefty bulge there. If a climax like that *did* ease the pain of a spanking, it was well worth enduring punishment on a regular basis. When she'd come it had nearly blown the top of her head off.

Her eyes flicked to Julian's and he waggled his sandy brows at her in a *get a move on* gesture. Alice surveyed him serenely. She felt powerful now, as if that too was a byproduct of being punished. Had Mrs. Grayson experienced this? Or had she always been subservient to Mr. Grayson? He seemed to have ruled his household with a rod of rattan, but somehow that didn't seem quite the way for herself and Julian to conduct their relationship. She was too modern for that, and she sensed he wouldn't expect her to accept total subjugation—even if he'd wanted to enforce it.

"What are you thinking about, love?" His blue eyes glinted, and she admired the way that he seemed prepared to wait on her convenience now.

"Oh, just stuff." With a creamy smile, Alice sank to her knees before him, not in obeisance but to get at what she wanted—and what *he* wanted too.

Trying not to grab like a kid in a candy store, she attacked the button and zipper of his jeans. With care, she opened them up. He was so rampant. She didn't want to hurt him. There was pain and there was pain, and she loved her husband and his equipment very much. As if he were a most precious treasure in the world, some rare and prized gem from the market they'd attended, she eased him out into the cool air to admire him.

Penises were odd sorts of things, but Julian's had a bizarre beauty. He was rosy and veined, with a large, well-defined glans. Silky pre-come glistened on the taut, shiny skin and his love-eye was distinct, almost winking at her. She'd never seen anything more tempting in her life. Extending her tongue, she swirled it delicately around his tip, and garnered a harshly in-drawn breath for her efforts. "Oh Ali," he moaned as she parted her lips and slowly engulfed him.

Oh, he was so fine. His texture was smooth against her tongue, and his flavor so salty and raunchy. She swirled at him, sucking and teasing and reveling in the sounds of pleasure he uttered, and, as she redoubled her efforts, the elegant profanities he shouted.

"Oh, you beauty, you beauty," he growled, grabbing her head, his fingers digging into her hair. He was rough, but she could feel the tension in him. He didn't want to hurt her while she was pleasuring him, which was a fine irony after what he'd so recently done. Alice laughed around his flesh, and then attacked him even harder with her tongue, while wiggling her fingers into his jeans to cup his testicles and stroke his perineum.

"Oh, Jesus God, Ali!" It was Julian's turn to wail, his hips pumping as he filled her mouth with semen. He pulled her hair, holding her on him, but she barely felt it. She just caressed him and loved him, her heart swelling.

THREE

Later, they adjourned to the bathroom, and showered together, washing each other companionably. The wild events of the spanking and its aftermath seemed to have released all trace of tension and frustration. Temporarily, at least. They handled each others' bodies with care and tenderness, and Julian was particularly solicitous, particularly gentle when he soaped Alice's bottom. In fact he handled her as if she were made of spun glass.

"Don't worry," she said, kissing his wet neck as they stood against each other, "It barely hurts at all now. You don't have to treat me with kid gloves."

Perhaps a bit of an exaggeration—there were still twinges—but it was amazing how the first soreness had ebbed. Alice wondered again about Julian's experience, and whether it allowed him to spank without creating lasting pain.

Retiring to bed, they shared their wine at last. Julian had opened one of their better bottles, to mark the occasion, and Alice savored its rich, sophisticated bouquet, knowing she'd earned it. Lying naked on her stomach it was a bit awkward to drink from the large wine glass, but she managed. When she set it aside, it was time to ask the questions.

"You've done that before, obviously," she observed, reaching out to rest her hand on Julian's outstretched thigh. He was sitting up against the pillows, glass in hand, his eyes closed; but they snapped open at the sound of her voice.

"Yes, I have, but not for a while. Not since we met."

She believed him. Tiredness drifted down over her, and she almost didn't push it, but the spark of curiosity was just a bit too strong to be ignored.

"So, what happened before we met? You must have... well...done it quite a bit. I mean, I'm a complete newbie to it, but even I can tell you're very good, very skilled." She smiled encouragingly, and then looked beyond him to the little ledger that sat on his bedside table. "Maybe not quite on Mr. Grayson's level, but it's obvious you know what you're doing. How did you start?"

"When I was nineteen, and on my gap year, I spent a few summer months alone in our house with an old friend of my mother's who was sort of minding the place while Mum went on a cruise." Julian slid down to lie beside her, and Alice was glad of the little moment while he settled himself. Her husband had been into spanking and BDSM since his teens? Why had he never ever said anything?

"Margery was nice, and kind of sexy. She'd been in some kind of financial trouble and Mum had helped her out with a place to stay for a while. Anyway, one day when there were just the two of us in the house, I found a magazine...a spanking magazine." His blue eyes glittered and he grinned. "It really turned me on, even more than vanilla porn. I think Margery left it out on purpose to test me, to see if I was game." He paused, and settled his hand on Alice's back, right on the small of it, just above the margins of her still warm bottom. "And I was, and one thing led to another."

Alice wanted to look away, and absorb what she'd heard, but Julian's gaze was mesmerizing. It held her. She imagined him with another woman across his knee. A sexy, curvy middle-aged cougar who liked her bottom spanked, someone who was juicy and experienced and irresistible to a horny young man. A latter day Mrs. Grayson.

Did he still think of her? Oh Lord, did he still *see* her? Surely he had to have an outlet for his preferences, and he was thirty now, as Alice herself was. If he'd been getting together with this Margery for over ten years, what did it say about their marriage?

Julian's fingers curved against her skin, not quite caressing, but somehow speaking to her. "I know what you're thinking, love, and yes, I did see her, on and off, for a few years, even while she was involved with other men. We were fond of each other, she liked to be spanked and I liked to spank her. She wasn't getting that from any of her boyfriends."

"But you don't see her now?" She had to be sure, really sure.

Julian's fingers spread across her back, and the little one just feathering over the upper edge of her bottom cheek, where he'd spanked her. A plume of heat blossomed, not so much there as in between her thighs.

"No, when I met you and fell in love with you at first sight, I ended my arrangement with Margery immediately." His little finger went rub, rub, rub. Alice wanted to squirm. Was he trying to distract her? Was she even bothered if he did? She believed him utterly, she always had. He might have kept this from her, but she knew he wasn't a liar, not at heart. "I only wanted to be with you, and fortunately, as it happened, Margery had finally met someone else who wanted to spank her. A rich older guy. They're married now, Mum tells me, and they dote on one another."

"That's nice."

"It is. But I sense more questions." His fingers slid further and spread, until he was cupping her bottom cheek. The heat grew, but not from her spanking, she barely felt that. No, it was the fires of desire that burned now, despite her curiosity.

"But haven't you missed it? The spanking games, I...I mean." He was squeezing now, very lightly but it was impossible to ignore. "You just don't forget about something like that, surely? I know I wouldn't."

Julian's eyes were steady. So was his voice. "No, I haven't really missed it. Except perhaps very occasionally..." She believed him. He was her husband. She trusted him. "But right from the start, the sex between you and I was so great—*is* so great—that it's always satisfied me completely." His fingers flexed, the action barely perceptible. "Now and then, the thought of it might have crossed my mind. But you and I met and then married so quickly. I didn't want to spring it on you that your new husband was a pervert. I just knew the right time to reveal it would come eventually. When you were ready..."

Alice's heart thudded. It was more than desire she felt now, much, much more. Julian had suppressed his needs for her sake, so as not to frighten her. Her soul seemed to roll over inside her, moved by his care and thoughtfulness.

"You should have said something, love. I'm not a completely vanilla person either. I have kinky thoughts. Fantasies, you know?"

Julian edged a little closer to her, his fingers tightening on her bottom, and below, his newly erect shaft nudging her thigh. "In that case, I'm bloody glad I caught you fondling that cane on the market stall. Hell, I wanted to shout for joy. I got a raging hard-on right there and then. I could tell by the way you handled it, and your body language, that you understood straight away."

"You were watching me?"

He grinned. "Well, yes, but just for a few moments. I was looking for you and I came around the corner of that row of stalls and saw you with the cane. I was just going to come up to you, and then I saw you running your fingers along it, and bingo, Bob's your uncle, I was erect. And I knew you'd notice, so I hung back and thought I'd wait, to make sure." His grip on her bottom tightened into a fierce caress, and Alice was compelled to press her groin against the bed. Julian's eyes glinted as he noticed it. "And afterwards, when I headed for the stall myself and studied the inventory of that box, and found you'd bought the punishment ledger. Well, it was all I could do not to jerk myself off when I got to the car." He shifted his own hips, pushing himself against her. "It took a massive effort of will to make that hard-on go down, I can tell you. It nearly killed me to wait until later, when we got home, to broach the issue."

Alice wanted to speak, to ask questions, but she was unable to. Julian's fingertips were playing in her anal groove now, and his other hand had sneaked in beneath her belly, heading for her sex.

"So," he said as he found his goal, "do you think you like it? Being spanked, that is? Or was that just a one off?"

Alice was almost choking with lust and gathering pleasure. Her husband's fingertip circled and rubbed. "Oh...Oh, I do like it. I like it a lot," she gasped, "Don't get me wrong, I don't want to give up ordinary sex altogether. But, well, I'd like to play spanking games some of the time, too."

She ground her hips, pressing down on the clever digit that was pressing up between her labia. Her sex rippled. Her silky fluid coated his fingers. "I'd rather like to see what my limits are. That is, if you can accommodate me."

"You're a bold one, Mrs. Porter, and a very kinky woman." His voice was different now, and it seemed to ring with authority, even though he spoke softly. Tormented by his fingers, Alice moaned, almost coming as he played with her anus.

"Are you going to spank me now?" she asked in a high, strained voice, not quite knowing what she wanted herself. She only knew that she did want something. Soon... "I need to come."

"And so do I, greedy, wicked girl," said Julian with a low laugh, "I don't know whether to tan your hide, or shag you senseless." He slid his fingertip teasingly away from the heart of the matter, while at the same time teasing the groove of her bottom.

Alice groaned, hiding her face in the pillow, biting it in frustration. She wanted to nudge Julian's finger back onto her center, but he was in charge now. She had to behave and wait for his whim. But she let out a high squeak as he toyed with her vent.

"Dirty, disgusting little trollop," he taunted, his voice warm with love, "I think I'll do both. A few hard spanks might tame your lewd desires, and then I'll give you a damn good seeing to and relieve the erection you've caused."

In spite of the tormented state she was in, Alice giggled. Julian was playing at being Mr. Grayson again now, acting the role of the horny patriarch disciplining his wayward wife.

"Oh, so it's funny, is it?" he demanded, giving her bottom just one last tickle and then rising up, onto his knees beside her. His shaft bounced as he moved, and as Alice twisted her head to see what he was doing, she let out another giggle to see it up and swinging.

"You're willful and disrespectful, Mrs. Porter." Grasping her thighs, he parted them, and then edged a bit further down the bed, to get the right angle. "Hold onto the bedstead, and then come up onto your haunches. Present yourself for the punishment you deserve."

Alice shuffled to comply, resting her forearms on the pillow, her head between them.

"Tut-tut. Thighs wide apart and back dished. That's better. Show what you've got."

Alice thrilled as she moved, adjusting her position. She'd never felt so slutty or debauched in her life, but she loved it, exhibiting herself for Julian this way.

"You're a lascivious wench, my darling. I can see your juice running right down your leg, you atrocious woman." A single fingertip slid into her cleft from behind, drifting over her perineum, then poking into her channel, pressing in and stirring her until she hissed between her teeth.

Oh Julian, do something, please! Slap me, have me or play with me, whatever...but please, please, do something. The plea was silent, but Alice couldn't keep still as Julian pumped her with his finger. She clenched her inner muscles, trying to grab him, ashamed that the action would make her anus wink at him.

"Right. That's it. Now I'm going to spank you very hard, and then I'm going to have you."

The words, just the words, almost made her come, but before her body could obey its own imperative, Julian whirled his hand away from her and brought it down again, hard on her bottom, once, twice, and really hard. The shock threw her forward against the pillows and her buttocks flexed and seemed to burn, the fires alight again.

Alice mewled against the pillow, churning her hips, seeing crimson behind her closed eyelids. More spanks fell, and she found herself lifting her bottom, pushing up, pushing back, and enticing her husband to slap her harder. She wiggled her burning rump in order to goad him.

Julian growled at her, regaling her with a few words and rebukes that Mr. Grayson would probably have never uttered, but which sounded like pagan music to Alice's ears and drove her to even greater efforts to lure him.

"Do you want the cane? Is that what you want?" he hissed into her ear, and in that heartbeat Alice realized it was exactly what she wanted, no matter how awesome and how agonizing it's power was.

"Yes, I bloody well do!" she cried defiantly. "Bring it on!"

Julian slid off the bed for a moment, searched around beneath it and then popped back up again. Alice glanced towards him, her hips still swaying, and saw the forbidden treasure in his hand.

You devil! You had the cane under the bed all along.

"Now brace yourself. This will hurt like hell," he said in a low, tight voice as if he were struggling to control himself, "But I'll give you something nice afterwards, almost immediately, to soften the pain."

Gritting her teeth, with her heart pumping and pounding and her spirit soaring, Alice dished her back as deeply as she could, making the best possible target.

"Good girl, good girl," praised Julian, pausing to slide a hand beneath her and feather a finger over her sex, "Good girl," he repeated, withdrawing and raising his arm.

There was a sound half way between a swish and a whistle, and then...nothing. No sensation at all for a heartbeat or two, and then a high white jolt of excruciating electric agony, right across the under-hang of her bottom.

Alice didn't scream. She hadn't the breath. She was rigid with shock. Then a second later, she howled out loud and grabbed her bottom.

"Oh no, no, no, I'll deal with that." Julian prized her fingers from her own flesh and conducted them back to the bed rail, curling them around it.

Oh, it hurt, it hurt. Alice rocked her hips, circling her bottom around, flexing the abused muscles and clenching her sex at the same time. The stripe from the cane was like pure flame, but her emptiness was worse, far worse.

She crooned like an animal when she felt Julian push inside her, thrusting in right to the hilt and knocking against the weal from the cane's descent with the base of his belly.

"Oh God, Alice, I love you!" he cried, jamming into her again and again and again, out of all control. Every wild shove knocked the root of her pleasure from within, and before she could draw breath, Alice was climaxing as never before, her inner muscles clamping and grabbing with love at her husband's penis.

When he reached around and touched her, she did scream then.

FOUR

For the second time that evening, Alice lay on the bed on her front and propped up awkwardly on her elbows. This time she was quite sore, there were no two ways about it, but the cooling muscle rub that Julian had just applied was helping a little bit.

Still Alice smiled. Every pulse and throb was a sweet reminder. Not just of the spanking, and the cane, but the heights of ecstasy she'd shared with Julian straight afterwards.

Good grief, if that happens every time, it's more than worth it. She grinned as she studied the old ledger that was open on the pillow before her, at a brand new page.

There was a new entry too, in modern ink that somehow looked quite at home on the antique paper. It was headed *Mrs. Alice Porter*, and the handwriting was Julian's —a neat but profoundly masculine script.

This evening, I found it necessary to discipline my dear wife Alice for her continued and willful extravagance, a fault I have taken her to task for on many occasions to no avail. With no other action left to me, I was forced to take down her jeans and panties and put her across my knee for a stringent and extended hand spanking. During the course of this somewhat lenient expression of my displeasure, my dearest did struggle and yell in a most unseemly and ungrateful manner and even derive a lewd enjoyment from her punishment. So much so that it was necessary to stop her mouth in a most particular way, to silence her cries.

Alice's smile widened to a creamy smirk. Well, that was one way to describe a blowjob.

Subsequently, it later became necessary to position Mrs. Porter on the bed, and administer an additional punishment, including a sharp cut with our newly purchased cane, as the first chastisement had not induced an adequate state of remorse or repentance. It is my hope that this additional disciplinary action will ensure Alice's compliant behavior for some time, perhaps as much as a week? It has certainly lent a most appealing coloration to her bottom.

"Bastard," Alice muttered fondly, reaching around to touch the cane's harsh kiss, and making herself gasp and squirm anew at the sharp sensation.

Flipping back to earlier entries in the ledger, she wondered if Mr. Grayson had left out the same things Julian had left out. She had a strong suspicion he'd perpetrated the same omissions; descriptions of the palliative fondling during, and the violent, delicious couplings that had occurred after the punishments. She only hoped that Mrs. Grayson had been the beneficiary of those pleasures even when it had been the maid, the cook or the governess who had received the spanking.

A small sound close by made Alice halt her musings, and as the bathroom doorknob turned she closed the ledger and pushed it away. Julian said nothing as he entered the room and closed the door behind him, but his eyes were aglow with happiness and with love. When he slipped off his dressing gown, he still really didn't need to speak at all. His splendid body was far more eloquent than any words, and it told her in no uncertain terms that the sight of her chastised bottom had a powerful effect on him.

Oh yeah.

As her husband smiled, Alice smiled too. Then, while he climbed onto the bed beside her, she fingered her weal again and pushed her hip against his thick, rampant penis, already wondering what might be described in the *next* ledger entry. It wouldn't be about tonight though. Keen as she was, she'd had her fill of the cane for moment.

For now, she'd be perfectly happy with what came afterwards.

IN SEBASTIAN'S HANDS

INTRODUCTION

In Sebastian's Hands is a trio of short stories about feisty, inquisitive Megan Chambers and her deliciously dominant lover, Sebastian Holmwood.

Life the Universe and Sebastian describes their first meeting, at a fancy dress party, when Sebastian initiates Megan into the mysteries of BDSM.

It's Time finds the pair as an established item, delving deeper into pain and pleasure as their relationship also grows in intensity.

The Roses in Your Cheeks is a story celebrating the fact that Megan and Sebastian are together forever, enthusiastically continuing their erotic spanking games as a happily married couple

LIFE, THE UNIVERSE AND SEBASTIAN

He was the most unusual looking man at the party. Even in a room full of Batmen, Supermen and cowboys he stood out. His long, pale face, his peculiar silvery blue eyes, and his curly black hair did remind me vaguely of an actor I rather lusted after on the television, but he didn't seem to be in fancy dress like the rest of us. Unless his shirt, jeans and jacket in unadorned black stood for something of which I wasn't yet aware.

"Hello, who are you supposed to be?" I enquired, with all the boldness of two sizeable gins inside me as I zeroed in on him across the crowded room.

"I'm just myself, I'm afraid," he replied, his voice amused and quite distinct despite all the hubbub, "Sebastian Holmwood. At your service." He paused, cocked his head a little on one side, and gave me an appraising look, "Pleased to meet you Miss Peep," he said, holding out a narrow elegant hand towards me. "Would you like me to help you round up your lambs?"

I felt embarrassed. Not only by my Victorian nursery rhyme costume, but because I didn't have a free hand with which to shake his. I had a glass clutched in one, and my so called "crook" in the other; a sort of cut-down affair made of yellowish rattan with a blue bow tied round the curly end. This object had come with the costume, but looked more like a school mistress's cane to me than anything, and certainly nothing like a shepherding implement.

Sebastian Holmwood looked at me expectantly, then quirked one fine dark eyebrow. Shaking his head slightly, he first relieved me of the glass, and put it aside, then drew the crook from between my suddenly sweating fingers.

To my surprise, he didn't abandon it straight away, as he had done the glass, but ran a forefinger slowly along the length of it. There was an odd expression on his face as he handled the long, yellow stick, something I couldn't define. It sent a delicious yet icy shiver down my spinal column. The look in his eyes was far away, almost dreamy. Feeling uneasy, I held out my empty hand.

"Megan Chambers. How do you do?" I said.

As if loath to tear his attention away from the crook, Sebastian offered his right hand, his left still curved around the rattan.

"I do well, Megan," he said, with an oblique playful smile, "And I soon hope to be doing much better." He glanced down at the crook, balanced across his fingers, and then passed it back to me with a hint of reluctance.

Cheeky sod!

The fact that I'd been so obvious stung me. He knew I fancied him and he seemed to find that highly entertaining. And what was all that business with the crook too? He was still looking at it as I hung it from my sash and reached for my drink.

"Nice party," I murmured, resolving to invest only a few

further moments of small talk, and then move on to someone a tad less disturbing if not quite as attractive.

But it didn't happen that way.

In spite of our prickly beginning, conversation flourished and I soon found myself warming to Sebastian. His manner was wry and charming, with a quick effortless wit, and before long attractive became downright enthralling. Our chat started with jobs, mine as an admin clerk for a retail chain and his as a software development consultant. Then, we moved on to TV, books and films, and effortlessly progressed through hopes, fears and phobias, and right on to life, the universe and everything. The more we talked, the easier it was, and we both agreed that we were like fishes out of water in a frivolous, booze-sodden gathering like this with raucous, seeming atonal music and a lot of people shouting and some falling down. We both admitted we'd only turned up as a favor to our hostess because she'd been nervous about the party being a flop. I soon started to get ridiculously excited at a piece of information Sebastian imparted to me under cover of some ancient disco tune or other. His own flat was only two floors above us, in this large old converted Edwardian building.

We were trundling along beautifully, with me feeling more relaxed with a man than I had in a long time, even if I was a tiny bit scared of him too, when Sebastian's eyes narrowed at something or somebody he'd obviously just caught sight of right behind me. The look on his face was dismissive, almost contemptuous, as if what he'd seen deserved nothing but disdain.

Intrigued, I turned around.

One of our fellow guests, a girl I knew vaguely from work, stood giggling and swaying on very high heels, as she brandished what looked like a riding crop over the back of a man kneeling before her. "Go on, Doreen, whip him!" somebody cried out, and Doreen giggled even louder and tapped her victim with the crop. She was wearing a short leather skirt, fishnet tights, and a low cut red top made of some shiny nylon stuff. Affixed to her bosom was a large, ribbon trimmed rosette bearing the crudely printed legend "Miss Whiplash".

I turned back towards Sebastian, wondering why he disapproved of such a pathetic, but basically harmless spectacle.

The expression in his silvery eyes was more like pity now, and he was rubbing the very tips of his fingers together as if testing the texture of his skin. Questions surged to the tip of my tongue, but before I could ask them he said, "I've had enough of this. Come on, Megan, let's leave."

"What's wrong?" I enquired in the rather antiquated lift, fiddling with my crook because Sebastian seemed unsettlingly preoccupied.

"I..." He paused, watching me fidget, "Some people... They get ideas." He hesitated again, and then smiled, his eyes very bright and intense.

"What ideas?"

"You wouldn't understand."

"I might!"

He looked at me very steadily, very searchingly, his expression lit as if from a fire within. I sensed him thinking very carefully about something, weighing possibilities, and assessing me again, even more stringently than before. "You might at that," he conceded at length, as if I had indeed passed some kind of test. "Yes, perhaps I ought to give you a chance."

In spite of my protestations, he'd lost me again. I understood nothing. But I had a feeling I might be learning pretty soon, and that excited me and made me uneasy, in equal measures.

Sebastian's flat was just the opposite of the chaos we'd left, just as spacious, but elegant, spare and silently and beautifully tranquil. The room we ended up in was as much an office, or library as it was a sitting room, with a leather-upholstered settee, a desk, and quite a lot of well-stocked book cases. The air seemed to hum with knowledge, and with a quiet, civilized peace. As I crept around, awestruck, examining prints and the spines of his books, Sebastian fixed drinks and put on some music; a light, but very stately piece by Mozart.

I didn't drink neat whisky as a rule, but after a moment, I found myself enjoying it. Not to mention *needing* it. Sebastian had picked up my crook from where I'd left it on his desk, and he was twirling it slowly in his fingers.

It gave me a very peculiar feeling in my stomach to see him almost caressing the thing like that. His hands were very pale, yet they looked strong. The word "capable" sprang to mind. The weirdest thoughts began to pass through my imagination, and when he swished the crook through the air, then smacked it against his palm, the hairs on the nape of my neck seemed to stand up one after another, a phenomenon I'd never actually experienced before, and always believed was just an old wives' tale.

Blushing furiously, I looked away, then sat down on the settee and picked up a book from his coffee table. I flipped a few pages, attempting to cover my nervousness, and then realized I'd made a huge mistake.

Sebastian's beautiful coffee table volume was full of pictures of people being punished. Women being beaten, their bare white bottoms lifted up and offered to a variety of different implements and techniques. As I stared down at a woman being thrashed across a table with a cane, a huge light bulb came on in the space behind my eyes… and I finally understood about life, the universe and Sebastian.

"'Those people, downstairs at the party… You realize how very little they know, don't you?" he said, a heartbeat later, as if my revelation had been flashed up on a screen.

"I… I think so… I'm not sure." I looked down at the caned woman in the picture, then across at my crook, its length revolving slowly between Sebastian's pale fingers, its true nature not at all hidden by that absurd blue ribbon.

Anxiety must have shown in my face, because Sebastian laughed, very quietly and very kindly.

"Oh no, not with this," he said, taking a step towards me, still twirling the cane. "I would never start a girl off with a cane. And this," He paused, that look of distaste resurfacing on his stark, rather aristocratic features, "This 'thing', is quite unsuitable anyway." With a swift, ruthless gesture, he snapped my *faux* crook in two pieces, and then dropped it into the waste-bin beside his desk.

"A girl's education should always begin with the hand," he observed, making a steeple of both his hands before him at waist level, and then raising them to touch the very tips of his fingers to his lips. "The hand is intimate. The contact is skin to skin. There's no better way to gauge the effect of a smack, and thus modify the force of the next one." He looked at me evenly, his pale eyes unblinking and slightly narrowed, then he nodded infinitesimally. Like an android, I rose to my feet.

Mozart played on softly, but all of a sudden I was in a new and surreal dimension. Sebastian Holmwood could control me with the very slightest gesture, and as he walked smoothly towards the settee, then sat down just a yard or so away from me, I turned to face him, my head meekly bowed. He was lower than me, seated whilst I was standing, but in all things he had the upper hand.

"So, Megan Chambers, do you want to understand? Our friends downstairs are woefully ignorant. You know that, don't you?" He reached out, took hold of both of my hands, and then held them in one of his. He let his free hand slide lightly down my hip, tracing its approximate shape through my costume's fluffy petticoats. Sensing that he required it, I looked up and met his eyes, realizing he was a little older, and far wiser, than I'd originally thought he was. I nodded, knowing instinctively what I'd let myself in for, and feeling both fear and curiosity in equal parts.

"Good," he said with a thoughtful smile, then let his hand slip beneath my skirt and petticoats. "Are you wearing anything beneath these?" He plucked at the long, lace trimmed mock Victorian pantaloons that peeked out from beneath my hem, then flattened his hand, slipped it upwards, and cupped the rounded cheek of my bottom.

"N... No," I quavered as he squeezed. I'd expected to get the costume grubby at the party, and as I'd be laundering the whole thing anyway, I'd decided to be naughty and go without any extra knickers.

"Excellent!" His eyes gleamed. "Now lift up all these skirts up for me. There's a good girl." He released my hands and nodded to my Bo Peep dress and all the frippery beneath it.

"But..."

Sebastian didn't speak, but his cool old-fashioned look spoke volumes. Trembling, I reached for my hem, then hauled up my skirts and held the whole lot in a haphazard bunch at my waist.

"Back and front," he specified. I obeyed with a graceless scrabble, and then closed my eyes as he gripped my pantaloons, whipping them down to my knees with one smooth, efficient jerk.

"Lovely," he said softly. I could almost feel the weight of his gaze on the curly triangle of my sex, like a radiant therapy that made my hidden folds heat. "Now turn around for me."

Shuffling, I presented my bottom, keenly aware of its plump, curvaceous shape.

"Perfect." His voice was a whisper and I heard the leather upholstery creak as he shifted position. I was quite disappointed that he didn't try to touch me.

"Turn again."

I complied.

"Open your eyes."

Again, I did as I was told, aware that my whole face was one big blush.

Sebastian was sitting comfortably on the sofa, his posture strong-looking, his knees spread a little apart. "Do you know what to do?" he asked. The gleam in his eyes was like starlight.

I bit my lip. I knew, but I couldn't say it.

"Come on. It's easy. Come across my knee. I won't bite you."

I wasn't worried about him biting.

Slowly, cautiously, I laid myself across his lap, letting his hands guide me into exactly the right position. My balance seemed precarious, and I felt vulnerable and dizzy, with my head down and my bottom rudely up. I couldn't imagine how I'd let myself get into this pickle. What the devil had I been thinking of? One minute I'd been flirting lightly with a moderately attractive man; and the next I was face down across his knee, about to let him spank my bare buttocks. How could I have been so reckless, so foolish? How could I have been so completely insane?

The answer was that against all reason, I trusted Sebastian Holmwood; perhaps more than I'd ever trusted anyone in my life.

And I moaned like a wanton, as if it had been all my idea in the first place, when Sebastian started touching me.

"You have a remarkably nice bottom, Megan," he commented, oh so conversationally, like a wealthy connoisseur appraising an objet d'art. His fingers palpated the muscle of each of my bottom-cheeks in turn, pressing them firmly as if testing their resilience. "Firm flesh. Soft, pale skin. You'll mark very well, I think." His fingers slid dangerously downwards, between my legs, then retreated and settled delicately on the very crown of my left buttock. "Oh yes, my dear, I'm going to make you pink."

Thinking about my face, I was just about to remark that I was pink already. But instead I yelped like a startled puppy when the first spank fell.

Why had I imagined it would just be a mild tap? The full power of his hand was astounding. Earth shaking. I could swear that I felt every bit of the shape of it, four distinct fingers and the open palm, scorched indelibly into my right bottom cheek where it'd landed. My lungs filled, and I opened my mouth ready to howl a protest and stop things going further, but then he spanked again, and my brain couldn't function. The second smack singed my left cheek, making it a match for the other one, and already my eyes were filled with tears. Half-blinded, I reached around, driven by a natural instinct to protect my flesh.

"No," said Sebastian, soft and low, and the single word froze me to immobility. My bottom was tingling, glowing, twitching, yet I dare not move a muscle to try and soothe it.

Sobbing, I felt my two hands once more gathered in one of Sebastian's, then pinned gently, but with no nonsense, at the small of my back. I couldn't believe I'd only taken two strokes. It seemed like a hundred. But very soon those first two became nothing more than a memory, submerged in the growing flame that licked and seared across my buttocks.

The spanks landed briskly, methodically and without mercy. Despite feeling as if I was lost in some kinky wonderland, I could still sense Sebastian's excitement too. And admire his meticulous attention to detail. He was working his way around in a pattern, covering the entire surface of my bottom, making every bit of me hurt and turn red. While he belabored me, he talked to me constantly, his soft baritone voice unruffled and hypnotic.

As his palm and his fingers turned my skin and flesh to incandescence, he described the regime he would impose on me in future... if *I* chose it.

Spank! I would be taken across his knee regularly, for treatment like this, but considerably sterner.

Spank! I would be beaten with implements when I was a little more experienced, when my bottom and my temperament were better seasoned.

Spank! I would taste the strap, the hairbrush, the ruler. And I would cry.

Spank! I would be stripped naked, gagged and bound, and take the cane. The *real* cane, not that silly toy brandished "Miss Whiplash".

Spank! Spank! Spank! I would suffer, at great length, and I would endure. And afterwards my sweet reward would come.

By the time Sebastian's hand fell still, I was weeping freely, my mind a mass of shock and awe and wonders.

My bottom was a swollen, throbbing war zone. I

couldn't believe that anybody in their right mind would seek this condition more than once. It seemed ludicrous. Yet the thought of *not* following the strange path that Sebastian had laid before me was impossible, unbearable. I felt confused, out on a limb, and bereft of any purpose except sharing *this* with him. The idea of losing him, or displeasing him, could not be borne.

I whined pitifully when he turned me over on his lap, and the denim cloth of his black jeans chafed the soreness in my bottom. But some of it wasn't from the pain.

"There, that's better, isn't it?" he said, wiping away my tears, and then stroking my jaw line and my brow with infinite gentleness.

Better than what? I wanted to ask, but beyond the superficial question lay the answer my heart knew. I *did* feel better than before. I felt wonderful. Despite all the torment in my hind-parts, I felt completely relaxed and peculiarly at peace.

Back at the party, I'd been edgy, worried about meeting someone, and nervous about how I looked and facing the ever present struggle to make small talk. I'd felt competitive, combative, forced to assert myself and be part of a scene I wasn't really sure I liked at all.

Now I felt calm, serene, and detached from all my former fears. From this day forward, the only thing that mattered was doing well here, in this room, for Sebastian. Life was simple. My world was straightforward. All I had to do was to receive as much punishment as he could give, and he'd be pleased. I wanted to shower him with kisses to show I understood.

But I didn't need to. As I looked at him, his great silver-blue eyes shone, full of happiness. Just as before he'd read my feelings on my face.

"You've done beautifully, Megan," he whispered, "I'm very pleased with you. But I think you already know that, don't you?" With a low laugh, he shifted me on his knees and adjusted my position. As he kissed the groan of anguish off my lips, the proximity of certain parts of him to certain parts of me told a delicious and very unmistakable story.

"And now, my darling, it's time you had a treat for being brave," he said as he broke the kiss.

Then he grinned, and I grinned. We both knew I hadn't been brave at all.

But even so, he placed his hand between my legs, and then bestowed on me that sweetest of rewards.

It was the first of very many, that perfect night.

IT'S TIME

"Late again," says Sebastian, his silver-blue eyes glittering as he fingers his precious antique fob watch.

He loves that watch. He loves it in exactly the way I hoped he would. It was my gift to him, and time has become very important to us recently. It's like the steady beating heart at the center of our relationship; part of a set of conditions that give it weight and form and purpose.

And I love that piercing, metallic look of his, the one that comes over his face when I defy one of his temporal strictures. It has the power to make my heart thud like mad and my pussy quicken with desire. I see that expression unfailingly at the beginning of our erotic adventures together, and when it's there, I know my bottom is bound to suffer for my "crimes", real or imaginary.

"I'm sorry... I just got talking," I mutter, throwing down my bag on Sebastian's leather sofa, and getting an elegantly raised eyebrow for my slovenliness as well as for a grossly late arrival, "You know how it is."

"No... Actually, I don't," he replies, flicking open the

beautifully engraved watch, and eyeing the time, then looking up again with that significant facial cast.

Sebastian doesn't chatter. Sebastian doesn't even make small talk without a purpose or subtext. He never wastes a single second of his life, and even these few passing moments during which he silently admonishes me are full of meaning and a source of sly delight to us both. With his eyes squarely on me, unwavering and all knowing, I shiver and feel my knees begin to quake. I can clearly see the color of his plans.

"Time is a very precious thing, Megan," he says to me, quietly, his deep baritone deliciously exciting, "Some people say that it's the fire in which we burn. A predator which stalks us... And thanks to you, we two have lost an hour." Snapping the watch shut, he tucks it away in the pocket of his waistcoat. I notice he is wearing the black, elaborately embroidered one he often chooses on these occasions. It's all part of his dramatic image as the dour disciplinarian. I'd giggle but I know I'm not supposed to. "A cause for punishment, I would have thought, wouldn't you?"

It's on the tip of my tongue to point out that I would have been punished anyway, it's the very reason I'm here, but I hold my counsel, and merely intone a solemn "Yes".

"In that case, Megan, you may go to the bedroom and make the customary preparations," he continues, a tiny smile playing around his lush yet sculpted lips, "And in fifteen minutes I will join you, and then we'll talk."

I nod, trying to keep my face straight, and then turn to leave the room. At the door, I get an overpowering urge to stop and curtsey to him, his manner is so unrelenting and magisterial today. But as he'd probably decree such an action to be flippancy and a lack of respect for our game, so I decide to play it safe and just get out.

Fifteen minutes? Well, it's not a long time in real terms, but plenty long enough to set my every nerve end tingling and drive me into a paroxysm of lust. I must admit that I'm still profoundly in awe of Sebastian and the strange, dark things he does to me, still the trembling acolyte after all these months of hard pain and easy, joyous love. There's so much to it all that still remains a total mystery to me; so much enlightenment that lies ahead. But it's a journey as complex and as tempting as the man himself.

If I'm to be ready in fifteen minutes, I need to get a hustle on. I'll get a black mark against my name if I throw my clothes about, so I've to be as neat as I am quick in getting changed. But it's hard to concentrate in this quiet sunlit bedroom, a place where we've shared so much, reached such heights.

The first thing I perceive as I enter is the ticking of his mahogany long-case clock. Not my gift this time, but his to both of us. The second thing is the nightgown Sebastian has laid out on the bed for me, one of the voluminous old brushed cotton numbers he likes me to wear sometimes... when we're playing. I'd never wear it to sleep; we both sleep naked. But the gown is a symbol, a prop. It's a totem of domestic discipline; part of the ritual, sweet and soft and comforting; in contrast to the hard, hard punishment.

Stripping swiftly, I peel off my smart suit, my blouse, my underwear and my stockings, and then let the snowy gown slither down over my vulnerable nudity. Dashing quickly into the en-suite I look in the mirror and use cotton wool to remove my eye make-up, rubbing away the subtle paint with trembling fingers and a little cleanser from amongst the toiletries I keep here. I didn't used to wear suits and high heels and "power makeup" to the office, but since I first met Sebastian, you could say I've bettered myself. I've progressed far and fast in the company hierarchy. Bending my will to his has given me the strength to conquer others. Talking with him in the long, happy hours when we meet as equals has given me new perspectives, new confidence, new self-belief. His encouragement has made me able to soar.

But now it's time to lie down, and abandon all thoughts of forgettable, everyday trivia, and office nonsense. I have no exalted status here in this room, no authority, no clout; I'm simply Sebastian's willing plaything, a submissive subject of the darkling prince of punishment.

The venue for much delicious pleasure, this bed I call ours now is inviting and comfortable, spread with a soft, pristine throw of high-end white chenille. Settling carefully onto my front, I rest my cheek on one bent arm, and then reach down behind me to pull up my cloudy night dress. Sebastian's preference at these times is for a bare, untrammeled bottom… because exposure makes me penitent and humble.

What must I look like now, I wonder? I try to imagine the sight that would meet any casual intruder, and that *will* meet my prince.

The vision presented to the visitor is that of a moderately pretty girl lying on face-down on a bed, with her legs and her buttocks completely naked. He'd see that her hair is short and blonde and cut in a stylish layered bob, and that her skin, though normally pale, is slightly flushed. He might be quite taken with the contrast between the billowing white primness of her saintly cotton night-dress and the shocking nudity of her bare, unsheltered buttocks. My buttocks are well-rounded and a little bit plump, and divided by a deep and rosy groove, but I like them that way now. I feel good about my body these days, when once, I didn't. My thighs are sleek and firm, but also curvy, just how

Sebastian likes them for the ruler. Something I might well get for being such a hussy and wickedly eager with my sex all lewd and unruly and glistening. I'm as wet as if he'd touched me already, in fact as if he'd stroked me long and lovingly. The way he does...

From where I lie I can easily see the clock. The yellow afternoon sunlight slants across it like a baleful slash, and shows my first five minutes are up.

Bang on time, the door opens and closes and Sebastian steps lightly into the room, filling it with the odor if his delicious cologne. I'm facing the window, so he can't see me smile, thinking of him freshening up for me just as I have for him.

He pauses in silence for a moment, piling on the pressure. I bet he's smiling. He might even be touching himself. I try to imagine what he's going to say, and recall similar situations, similar moments. All this waiting is no more than an eye's blink in the grand and cosmic scheme of things, but with his hand, or his belt, or some other well-chosen implement, Sebastian could transform it into an eternity of torment. Only last week he said, "I'm going to cane you for fifteen minutes... and after that I'm going to play with you for five." I can almost feel the rod from just thinking about its hardness; almost taste its bite as it lands upon my flesh. Sebastian didn't stop until those fifteen minutes were finished, despite the fact that I carried on and struggled like a weak-willed ninny. I didn't really deserve what happened in the subsequent five, but I got it all the same and he was equally, if not more resolute. He kept on caressing me no matter how many times I came, and my flesh was incredibly sensitive afterwards.

But that didn't stop me coming again when he kissed it better.

Time... There are so many ways he uses it to tantalize me. Like now... when will he speak? When will he speak?

The leather of the old armchair in the corner of the room creaks as he sits down, and he takes in a long breath. Tiny sounds tell me he's getting comfortable. It takes a second or two. Is he uncomfortable? Has he got an erection? Will he punish me harder because that's my fault?

"So, it's time. What shall we talk about?"

His voice is calm, serene, very soft and low. It flows over me, imparting calmness to me too.

"I don't know. My mind is blank. I've been trying to meditate."

It's pert, and very cheeky of me to answer like that, but he likes me that way. He prefers a bit of "resistance", something to play off, rather than a perfect, bland submission.

He laughs. "Oh, I'm sure you have. Meditating, my arse... I'll bet you've been lying here having filthy fantasies."

I haven't, really, but if that's what he wants, that's what he shall have. I lick my lips, out of his sight, summoning some up.

"It... it wasn't so much fantasies as memories. I was thinking about some of the stuff we've done."

"Stuff? Our arrangements are 'stuff' to you?"

"You know what I mean."

He heaves a sigh. "Go on."

The way he says that makes me quiver. There's power in two little words.

"I was thinking about the time you ordered me to arrive at midday, and you thrashed me once straight away, then again, every hour, on the hour, when the clock chimed.

God, I was sore that day.

"And did you enjoy that game?" There's another rustle as he moves slightly. Is he wearing his silk dressing gown, I wonder. He sometimes does for our little sessions. I'd love to turn my head and look his way, but I know I can't.

"Bits of it... The bits that happened on the half hour... They were very nice."

"Indeed."

On the half hour, he'd been just as kind as he'd been cruel on the hour, stroking me to at least one towering orgasm, if not more.

"And what else do you like? What other happy times do you like to fantasize about? What other little tricks? Do tell me more."

I have to shuffle a bit on the bed. I'm really excited now. I know I shouldn't rub my pussy against the beautiful chenille, but I can't help myself. I just can't help myself. He's made me ache without even laying a finger on me.

"I like it when you ring me while I'm at work and tell me to stop what I'm doing and go to the cloakroom to play with myself."

Oh, that's a good one. I love that. It's a perfect counterpoint to being the perfect example of rising management material that *he's* helped me to be; a luscious secret to spice up the daily routine. I excuse myself, speed to the ladies' room, and when I'm there, I have to stand in a cubicle for five minutes, with my skirt pulled up to my waist and my panties around my ankles, fantasizing about a pre-decreed image while I stroke my pussy.

"Really? I'm so glad you enjoy that. Tell me... what are your favorite images? What are the ones that are most likely get you off in five minutes?"

Most likely? Hell, I *always* get off. There hasn't been a single time, when, knowing I'm masturbating to his order, I haven't had to bite my lips to contain my moans of pleasure while a workmate or two pee or powder their noses, only feet away.

"Sometimes I think about you whipping me with a riding crop, while I'm bound across the trestle... without any clothes on." He doesn't make a sound, but in my mind I hear a grunt of satisfaction or even the little exhalation of breath when he lands such a blow. "Or I imagine myself draped across the back of the big armchair, and you're spanking me with one of your leather soled Persian slippers. And no matter how much I cry, you won't stop. You keep on going until your arm is really tired and then you get your cock out and you-"

"Yes, yes, that's quite enough of that. Go on... more about the punishments, if you don't mind."

I can't see him, but I can see the clock. I seem to have been talking for hours, but it's only a few minutes. Barely any time at all, he hasn't laid a finger on me, and there's already a little damp patch beneath me, where I've got sticky and aroused and seeped through the cotton of my nightgown and onto the perfect surface of the throw.

I can't help but think about other ideas he's seeded in my mind. Just remembering them makes my sex ache even more.

"Sometimes I imagine being at a party... not like the one we met at. It's more of a 'special' party where I'm the star attraction and you punish me in front of an audience, or let other people punish me while you watch them."

"Sounds interesting. Kindly expatiate."

I don't laugh but I want to. He uses big words sometimes where smaller ones would do. He's a very educated man... as well as supreme master.

"Well, it's all men, and me. And each one of them has fifteen minutes to do what they want with me... under your supervision, of course." He'll like that, more "time" involved.

"The first one is a teacher or something and he makes me bend over as if I'm at school and clasp my ankles. Then he takes my skirt and slip, and pins them up securely. To... to... expose me."

"Completely?"

"Um... no. He lashes me with a rubber 'slapper', but he lets me keep my panties on, the white lace ones you really like. Those ones we bought in Paris, you know?"

"I do know." He sounds stern, but I know he's only faking it. He puts on this very rigorous voice, but I know him. I can hear the laughter, beneath. He's just loving all this. "I just can't believe you'd show your very best knickers, that I bought for us alone, to some stranger, some teacher you barely know."

"I'm sorry."

"You'd better be. Pray go one."

"It hurts a lot, and I nearly fall over, and I cry a lot and it feels as if my bottom's all swollen. Then afterwards he makes me drop my knickers to show everybody there how red I am." Oh God, it's nearly killing me that I can't touch myself. I'm going crazy. Frustration plagues me far harder than any spanking. "And they all laugh because my knickers' crotch is so sticky and they know how turned on I am."

"Well, that's hardly surprising. You have no self-control whatsoever." It's not the truth. I actually have loads of self-control, thanks to Sebastian, but I know he's only teasing me. "What next?"

I hesitate a moment. I wish he'd let me look at him, but I've got to remain as still as I can, with my face towards the window and the chest of drawers with the little clock on the top of it. In my mind's eye though, I see Sebastian, lounging in his chair, looking wonderful and so handsome he's almost edible, with his dark hair, his lean strong body and his long elegant hands. In a private act of defiance, I picture him naked, his skin pale, but his cock rosy, and also long and elegant.

"Megan?" he prompts, and it's a slip, a personal touch. My inner turmoil increases, but in my heart now, not just my body.

"The next man has a go at me, and amazingly, it's that man off the television that I fancy. You know the one, the guy in the cop show who used to be a fake psychic? I don't know how he's at the party, but it's him and he's into BDSM, even though you wouldn't think it from looking at him on the box..."

"And moving on to the real point, please?" He's not cross. He doesn't really make any effort to hide his amusement. My crush on the television guy is a running joke between us.

"He was really strict, and he made me walk around the room with my knickers at half mast, to shame me. Everybody was looking at me, getting off on my embarrassment and the awkward way I had to walk. Especially you..." I'll probably suffer for that, but what the hell. "Then he took me across his knee and spanked me very hard for quite a long time. My bum felt like it was in flames, because of the rubber slapper. He covered every inch. I knew my cheeks were bright red. It was frightful. I thought he was a nice guy until then, but he was a real tartar."

"And did this treatment turn you on? Did you feel randy because it was your hero?"

"I was turned on because you were watching." It comes out without pause for any thought. It's the truth.

"I'm touched. Continue."

"There was only one more man who wanted a turn. He was older, and some sort of aristocrat, with silver hair and weird blank eyes... very cruel, even more than the others. His voice was very cold and he sounded weary and a bit bored with it all. He ordered me to remove all my clothing then made me climb up on the table, and then he thrashed me with a switch."

Sebastian says nothing, but I can almost hear him thinking, fantasizing just like me. I hear a rustling. I'm almost certain he's touching himself now, almost certain he's got his beautiful penis out. Oh, if only I could *see*!

When he still says nothing, I go on. "He's a consummate disciplinarian, very cruel. He lined up his cuts with almost mechanical precision, and then kept going back to the sorest places, just to make things worse. I was whining and complaining by the time he eventually finished with me, but my pussy was dripping, dying to be touched."

"Oh dear God..."

It's a gasp, almost a sigh of desperation. I've reached his limit, and my own. Defying his strictures, I roll onto my back just as he strides towards me. His cock is out, high and hard, bouncing wickedly as he lunges at me. Within a heartbeat, he's kneeling at my side, and he pushes me back onto my front, holding me down with one powerful hand on the small of my back, while he pumps himself, looming over me.

Still I strain to look at him, twisting to see him over my shoulder and loving the flush of pink on his razor cheekbones as he masturbates furiously. It takes but a moment or two for him to come heavily, his semen spurting and landing warm on my as yet unpunished bottom.

"Oh God... oh God, you're devil woman," he pants as he finishes, his chest heaving and his beautiful eyes almost rolling up in his head, "What you do to me... it's... it's amazing."

The sight of him amazes me. He's so wonderful, so wild, so revealed to me. I'm almost beyond sex, but at the same time drenched in it. I reach beneath myself, find my clit and rub it furiously.

But Sebastian is astonishing, he recovers in an instant, pitching forward, almost covering me with his own body while he too fishes beneath me, knocks my own hand away and starts rubbing me. He's all over the place; he must be still fazed by his orgasm. But still he manages to work me just how I like it, hard and fast and rough, almost hammering my clit with his fingertip.

I come immediately, I'm so excited. I thrash hard, flailing about clutching at him where I can reach him, behind me. His sticky cock is jammed against my thigh as I shout his name, soaring, dying... loving.

Afterwards, while I'm still in a dazed glow, he finally does spank me, warming my buttocks thoroughly and efficiently in the time honored way, and making me squeal even though I barely have a voice.

"Oh my darling," he murmurs, a moment or two later, sliding his hand beneath my belly to raise me up so he can fuck me.

When he pushes into me, my tears start to flow, but it's not from the pain. I'm crying with happiness, and so is he. We're in pieces with love.

"I think it's time," he says a few minutes after our mutual climax, while we're lying like spoons and he's warming his hard, flat belly against the heat in my sticky, pulsating bottom.

"Time for what?" My brain isn't really working properly. What is he talking about? Have I missed something somewhere?

"For us to take the next step."

My heart thuds hard. Does he mean what I think he means, or is it just some new level of refinement in the way we play our games together?

"Megan? Are you listening?" He kisses the back of my neck and I realize I've been hesitating.

"Yes... but I'm not sure what you mean." I am sure, actually. I know, suddenly in my heart, that it *is* what I think it is.

"Oh, I think you do..." His arm tightens around me. His voice sounds just a little bit tense, as if there's a crack in his confidence, a fear of my answer. "But it'll mean you giving up all hope of having a chance with your guy from the telly, or all those other men you fantasize about."

Despite the way he's holding me, I turn in his arms, not even wincing when my throbbing bottom plagues me. "They're only daydreams, Seb. The only man I really want to spank me is you... You know that." I touch his face, and kiss him lightly to eradicate any possible doubt. "You're a cruel brute sometimes, with a heavy hand, but I can't help but love you."

He laughs. He knows I'm joking and the only cruelty he wields is beautiful to me.

"And you're willful and defiant and sometimes you're a terrible submissive, but I can't help but love you too." He's joking too, I know that. Except for the very last element...

"Very well then, lover boy, it *is* time. If that next stage of yours is the one I'm thinking of too."

"Yes! Yes, it is!" he growls happily in my ear, and grabs me hard and close. I barely notice my twinges of pain as he kisses me like fury.

It's time for my friend and master to become my husband too.

THE ROSES IN YOUR CHEEKS

"But it's freezing outside... Are you sure you want to go out for a walk?"

Sebastian gives me one of his looks, his very significant looks, as he folds up his newspaper in the sitting room of the Rook's Nest Inn, where we're staying for a bit of a mini break. We haven't been away for quite a while. The last time was our luscious honeymoon in the Caribbean, but that feels like a lifetime ago now. That's the trouble when you get promotion at work. It becomes harder than ever to take a holiday when you want to.

"Absolutely," he says briskly, unwinding his tall lean frame from the chintz armchair. Even now we're so familiar with each other, I still almost gasp at the instant pang of lust. He's so strong, so powerful, and so dominant. "It'll put some roses in your cheeks, my love. You're looking a bit peaky... you could do with the fresh air." With no further ado he reaches for my hand and leads me out of the room, and away from the cheerful fire I was enjoying.

Not that I don't expect to enjoy myself elsewhere.

Roses in your cheeks.

With Sebastian, that doesn't mean my face.

The Rook's Nest Inn is a lovely old place, quaint and pretty and surprisingly well appointed for so small an establishment so off the beaten track. But alas, the way it's been renovated to provide for guest bedrooms and en suites, some of the walls are terribly thin. So much so that it's easy to hear the sex lives of the guests staying next door to us; and for them to hear us when we're at it.

So, no fierce and extended spanking sessions with me moaning and wailing and blubbering. No telltale "whack" of the slipper, the slapper or the cane.

And it's killing us. No wonder Sebastian wants to get out for a while. I can see the tension and the fire in him as he strides towards the staircase in reception, and feel it as he hustles me up the stairs ahead of him. His hands settle on my bottom to hurry me upwards, and I have to bite my lip, I feel so tense and so bloody yearning too.

It's not natural for me to go for more than a couple of days without those roses in my cheeks.

We scurry about our room, getting our things together. I desperately want Sebastian's hands on me, whether to punish or to pleasure, but I can hear our neighbors fussing next door, and if he and I start anything we're bound to be overheard.

When I slip into the bathroom to check my face and hair, I'm almost shaking. Almost fainting with lust. I've already got a bit of pink in my cheeks, and when I unfasten my jeans and slip my hand into my panties, I'm streaming wet. Sebastian can do that to me with just hints, and looks, and a lift of one elegant dark eyebrow.

I can't wait to bend over and yield my bottom to his hand.

When I leave the bathroom, he's waiting for me, looking impatient and already wearing his long, dark Belstaff overcoat. He springs up from the armchair as I reach for my own coat, and stays my hand.

"Just a minute... Let's make this walk a bit more interesting, shall we?"

Isn't it going to be interesting enough already, if he has in mind what I think he has in mind? What I pray he has in mind, regardless of the cold?

Oh... oh... I think it's the sex toys again.

"Sit down in the chair. Pull down your jeans and panties," he instructs me. His voice sounds crisp and businesslike, but his silver blue eyes are on fire. As I comply, shaking, he fishes in the pocket of his coat and draws out an item.

A confection of balls and silk cord.

It seems incongruous, in the man who is my master, but he sinks gracefully down and kneels beside where I'm sitting. There's nothing subservient about it though. He's simply down there for better access. Without so much as a by your leave, he rummages in my fleece and sticks a finger rudely inside me.

"Well, I thought we might need lube, but you seem to be saturated, dearest," he observes, then shoves in another finger. I groan. I can't help myself, and he murmurs, "Hush! The neighbors..."

And he's right. They're moving about in there, arguing by the sound of it. I don't care what they're up to or whether they hear me. I only stay quiet because Sebastian compels it. Riding his hand, I bite my lips and reach down to try and rub my clit, fingers close to his.

"Uh oh," he says quietly, shaking his dark curly head. "No pleasure for you just yet, naughty girl."

Withdrawing his fingers abruptly, he pushes them into my mouth now, and I lick them clean, loving my own foxy flavor. Then he whips out a snowy handkerchief to dry them... and sets about me again with the objects from his pocket which he'd placed to one side.

"Right. You know the drill. Knees apart, ankles together. Push up. Open yourself wide."

Breathing heavily I obey him, lifting my hips as best I can, and displaying my pussy.

Sebastian seems to consider lube again, but after a moment, he just presses the first of a pair of Chinese love balls against my entrance and shoves it into me without pause or mercy. It's quite a big one, quite a stretch, and my fingernails gouge the chair arm as he pushes it home, following up immediately and just as uncompromisingly with the second.

I'm stuffed. Beleaguered. Filled up. Bulging. How on earth will I be able to walk, feeling like this?

I gasp, hardly able to contain myself, but he gives me a firm look and I clamp my teeth together. I suppose I should be grateful that he hasn't put a plug in my bottom too, but the moment I think of that the perverse side of me wishes he had!

"Come on, let's go for that walk," he says briskly hauling me out of my chair and reaching for my coat. I'm barely on my feet before I'm panting hard, wracked with sensation as the balls roll and rock. "Hurry up, Megan... Let's get out of here," he admonishes, just as if there's absolutely nothing out of the ordinary and we're simply doing what most couples staying at a nice country inn do; which is, going out for a simple, pleasant walk.

He helps me into my coat and scarf like a devoted valet assisting his exalted employer. He treats me like cut glass, but all the time he's hiding a smirk at the thought of what's going on inside me. The way the balls roll and tilt makes me hot, and all of a flutter. I doubt if I'll feel the cold with all this heat on the boil.

Descending the stairs has me gasping. I try to walk as if on eggshells, and keep my face straight. Sebastian is all smiles. He thinks it hilarious. When we stroll through the lobby, he passes the time of day with the old ladies staying here. They think he's adorable, because he's good mannered and beautifully handsome with his black hair and his gleaming eyes. They seem to think he's an angel, a Botticelli angel. They'd probably have apoplexy if they knew what sexy perverted devil he really is.

The walk up the hillside path is pure hell. Sebastian strides out, holding me tightly by the hand, and makes me hurry after him. The balls roll and jiggle inside me, tugging and rocking against nerve endings, creating an agony of pleasure that plagues me all the more because I know there'll be another agony on the horizon. Well, perhaps not agony, but a ferment of heat and torment in my buttocks.

I'll burn, oh yes I'll burn, with fires both without and within.

Sebastian is in a rush. Having to contain himself in our very proper little country hotel has been driving him crazy. Not being able to make me moan and squeal, not being able to rock the bedstead as he fucks me to oblivion has been as frustrating for him as not having sex at all.

We've had to fuck on the floor, to keep things quiet, although it's probably not a good thing for my tormented body to think about that right now. He's gagged me so he could plague me with pleasure. He's plowed me furiously, biting his own lips to keep in his grunts and moans.

"There, what did I tell you? The fresh air has brought

roses to your cheeks," he says triumphantly as we reach the top of the hill, and he stops to give me a passionate kiss. It's very chilly out and we haven't seen anyone on the path. Sebastian takes advantage of that flip open my coat as clasp my crotch through my jeans. The pressure makes me pant and make the most uncouth noise, not to mention almost helplessly climax.

Almost...

I wriggle in his grip, trying to reach the pinnacle. My clit trembles, and my sex is awash with silky arousal.

"Naughty, naughty... you haven't earned that yet." He kisses me hard again, plunging his tongue in my mouth, subduing me. I wish he'd put his hand inside my knickers and stroke me, but I know I've got to pay my dues yet.

But where will he do the deed? Where will he punish me, out here, in the cold? There's still nobody about, but we're still out in public.

Sebastian's kisses are intoxicating. He's supremely good at it, as he is with everything else. Even if I didn't have a set of Chinese love balls inside me, and his strong hand clutching my pussy, I'd still be swooning from what he does with his nimble tongue and lips. Although I'm probably not supposed to, I reach up and cradle his beloved head in my hands, digging my fingers deep into his silky black curls.

He makes a low, admonishing sound in his throat, but goes on kissing; jabbing at my tongue with his own, then twirling the tip of his tongue around, tasting and teasing.

"What do you want?" he demands when our mouths break apart, "Tell me what you want... and I'll tell you what you can have." So stern. So thrilling.

"I want to come," I gasp.

"Just that?"

"I... I want to please you." It's true. I'd do anything for him, and endure any of his torments and games. Mainly because I know that in our real life, outside of this fantasy world we create for ourselves, he'd do anything on earth to make me happy.

"And what will you do to please me?" He's the one who sounds happy now, even though he's doing his best to put on his "fierce master" act.

"I'll bare my bottom so you can spank me and make me cry."

"An admirable sentiment, my love... but would you do it right here? Where we stand?"

I glance around anxiously, and he gives me a squeeze that makes me yelp. The path is deserted, but down below, on the lane that leads to the village, I can see people walking, braving the cold as we are. If he were to throw my coat up over my back, and pull down my jeans and knickers, there's nothing to say that any number of brave walkers wouldn't suddenly decide to ramble up this track.

And yet... it's so exciting. My pussy flutters are the thought of being found, so deliciously exposed in a public place. Especially so if my husband has put roses in my cheeks by the time they arrive.

"Yes. Yes, I'd do it here, if you wish it."

Sebastian laughs, and it's a husky thrilling sound. "I bet you would too, you trollop. I bet you'd enjoy showing yourself off to all and sundry... you fantasize about it often enough, judging by the tall stories you tell me all the time."

It's true. We both have the best fucks ever when I tell him my outrageous erotic daydreams, and the topic of exhibitionism is always a winner.

We stand, frozen in time, while he decides if we should

really take a risk. My hands are still upon him, one touching his hair, the other on his strong shoulder, so solid beneath the superb cloth of his Belstaff. He's still holding my pussy through my clothes, the pressure firm, reminding me of the unyielding balls inside me.

"Come on... let's walk a little further," he says, making a sudden decision which he marks with another rough squeeze of my crotch, before letting that go, and grabbing my hand to lead me along. I suppress my moans as he makes me hurry again, jostling the obstructions that rock against my womb.

A little way up the path, just over the brow of the hill, we come to a little stone structure, a sort of shelter for walkers to rest in, after the climb up, and enjoy magnificent views of the valley. The view isn't all that great today, as it's misty and foggy, but the shelter is welcome. Sebastian's grin tells me we've found the perfect venue.

"In there," he orders, hustling me in.

It's a strange, damp, gloomy little building, on this dim day. Open at the front, but with a wall, about waist high, and at the back there's a green-painted bench, a little worse for wear. Despite the fact it's so exposed and windswept, there's a suspicious odor of urine floating about. Ugh!

"You bring me to the nicest places," I mutter.

"Cheeky cow! The Rook's Nest isn't cheap you know," he counters. He's right; it's a very nice place, and quite exclusive. A real treat. "I'll have to punish you even more severely for your lack of gratitude."

As if you wouldn't anyway?

His pale eyes are glinting in the gloom, and just the sight of them affects my body. My sex clenches in longing, clamping down on the balls and making me gasp. Those eyes narrow as he perfectly reads my responses.

"And you're a horny minx too, aren't you? I bet you're wet through."

I refrain from pointing out that any woman with a tantalizing love toy inside her would be dripping. Not to mention having been kissed to within an inch of her life by the most gorgeous and most kinky man imaginable.

"Tell me. Are you wet?"

I'm quivering all over. He doesn't shout at me. He doesn't even sound cross or displeased. But somehow I'm a complete jelly of apprehension.

"Yes. Um... yes, master, I'm very wet."

"That's better," he says, approving the title. "I think we'd better inspect you now, hadn't we?"

I nod. I can't speak any more. I feel as if I'm going to explode with excitement and surging lust any second.

Manhandling me, Sebastian makes me lean forward, with my elbows on the low wall, my chin resting on my arms, and my bottom pushed out. Then, with no further ado, he throws my coat up over my back, and reaches around to unfasten my jeans. These, he drags hurriedly all the way down my legs to my ankles, taking my knickers with them.

I'm left standing there with my bum, my thighs and my legs all on show to whomsoever might amble past the shelter. The cold air feels like a dank film clinging to my nakedness, and my own moisture is so copious it starts to trickle down my inner thigh.

Sebastian tests me immediately, sticking two fingers peremptorily into my sex from behind. The tips knock against the Chinese balls inside me, and the balls in turn knock the root of my clitoris.

I make a gurgling sound and come a bit, clamping down on him.

"Dirty, undisciplined, intemperate girl," he hisses in my ear, rummaging around from the front for my clit and when he finds it, giving it a little pinch as it jumps. "You'll pay for that. I never said you could come, did I?"

"I'm sorry," I half stammer, half gulp; not feeling the least bit sorry at all. In fact I feel deliciously aglow and proud of myself and happy, and just dying for him to bring it on, and punish me.

He withdraws his fingers, giving the cord of the love balls a little tweak, but not pulling them out. The way they jump inside me makes me squeak, and nearly come again.

"Careful..." he warns, wiping his sticky fingers on my bare bottom. Oh, he's a prince. "I was going to just spank you, but because you're so willful I think we need a few refinements, don't you?"

Whatever, I think, but don't say so. I'm half off my head already.

Fishing around in his pocket, he gives me a baleful glare as I watch him out of the corner of my eye. He's clearly got some other fiendishness in there that I wasn't aware of, and it doesn't surprise me at all when he draws out our favorite set of nipple clamps.

"Oh no," I gasp, thinking, oh yes.

"Wicked little tart," he breathes against my neck as he reaches under me, pushing up my sweater and T-shirt right up, out of the way, and then unclipping the front fastening of my bra to free my breasts. My nipples are hard as little stones already, but he plays with them just a bit to be sure.

Then, the next torment begins. He screws first one clip in place then the other, and tears squeeze out of the corners of my eyes. They really hurt, and what's more, they're weighted, so they pull on breasts as they dangle. Worse, or perhaps better in a dark twisted way, that pulling sensation seems to drag my clit too.

What a state he's got me in. Here I am, presented, subjugated for his pleasure with a bare, vulnerable bottom and remorseless nipple clamps plaguing my breasts. I love it, being his "object", his plaything. My pussy drips. I'm almost ready to come, just from being here.

"Now stay where you are. Don't move a muscle. And most especially, don't touch yourself or climax."

Where's he going? Where the hell is he going? With a swish of his long dark greatcoat he strides out of the shelter and right out of view.

For a few minutes I'm completely alone. I'm fearful, yet absurdly, even more excited than ever. I imagine people, mainly men, coming along the path, and stopping to stare at my bum, and my breasts, perhaps fondling me. But I can't do a thing because Sebastian's told me not to move.

My heart nearly stops when I hear footsteps approaching, but then it speeds up even more when I recognize the tread. He swirls back into the shelter, a couple of freshly pulled and trimmed switches, mini branchlets, in his hands.

"These should do nicely," he says, sounding pleased with himself as he hefts the instruments of my forthcoming punishment, assessing their weight and flight like the expert he is.

Oh, those are going to smart! He's a master with any implement, and with his hand, but he'll really make those beauties fly.

"Have you moved while I was away?" He lays one of the switches across my bottom, just letting it rest there. "Have you fiddled with yourself, you naughty girl?"

I haven't, but part of me wants to say that I have. I love

playing the wicked, helpless, hopeless little strumpet to his stern disciplinarian.

"No matter..." He preempts my answer. "Even if you haven't done it, you've thought about it, and that's enough. The thought is misbehavior too." He reaches beneath me, tugging a nipple clip, and making me moan and jiggle my hips; which, of course, makes everything worse than ever, because of what's inside me. I really am in a terrible, yet wonderful state.

I'm dying to come again.

"Right, that's it... It's time to beat the wickedness out of you, you mucky little trollop." He taps my bottom ever so lightly, as if sighting for the real blows. "Assume a better position. You're not really trying here. Dish your back and stick your bottom out. Present yourself, woman."

I do the best I can, but it's difficult with my panties and jeans around my ankles, and it's cold too, even though I am burning up with desire.

Ow! Ow! Ow!

While I'm still trying to flex myself into a better shape for him, he lands three hard slashes, right across the crown of both buttocks at once, all parallel. After a split second of shock, they explode in white fire, and I keen out, "Nooo!"

"Yes!" he corrects, swishing again, another three.

Already sobbing, I rock my hips and that makes everything worse. The pain is fierce, but the love balls and the swing of the weighted nipple clips are demonic. I simply don't know if I'm coming... or going mad from the raging hurt in my bottom, and the torment of my breasts.

"Keep still, Megan. Be good. For me..." His voice is quiet, almost tender, sweetly beguiling.

I strain to obey him, and to please him. It's all I want to do right now. I have a real life, a normal life where I'm in control of my own destiny and I do what I want as a Twenty First Century woman, but in this precious magic world of ours, all I want to do, all I live for, is to be what *he* wants me to be.

His. His plaything. His object. His perfect submissive.

"There, that's better," he almost croons, punctuating it with another hard cut, right across the under-hang of my bottom, close to my sex. He would never hit me there, but getting within millimeters of it is a skill he's polished; that and striking me right across the vent of my anus... something he does now, in two sharp blows.

I'm crying freely now. My bottom is incandescent, agonized. But within, I'm rippling lightly around the solid spheres inside me as if I'm having a delicate, unstoppable, ongoing orgasm, fired by the pain.

Not being allowed to rub my clit is far more taxing to me than any amount of blows to my bottom.

I gasp. I gulp. I whimper. I'm not doing very well. I should really take this quietly. Sebastian belabors the sides of my buttocks and my thighs, spreading the heat and pain around. I wriggle and jerk, making the love spheres dance and the nipple pendants swing.

Suddenly, it's too much. I lose my head, and any semblance of control over my own sexual response. With a garbled cry... his name, I think... I surrender to a huge orgasm, and unable to stop myself I reach down and start fondling my clitoris in rough, hard strokes, working myself through it.

"Oh baby," Sebastian gasps, and the switch hits the floor. A heartbeat later, I almost faint when he wrenches the balls out of me by their cord and after an instant or two of rustling and fumbling... I'm filled again.

Stuffed to the brim with his hot, hard, dearly beloved cock...

"My darling, my darling..." he sighs, almost sobs into the back of my neck as he throws himself over my back like cloak of grace in his big, dark coat.

Sebastian, my husband, jams himself into me, again and again, in long, staccato strokes. It hurts where he's hit me, but I barely notice it. I'm still coming and it's better, infinitely better, than before. Especially when he reaches around, knocks away my fingers, and takes over in the pleasuring of my clit. He rubs me, circling and teasing and loving, somehow managing to stay exquisitely on target while he's half out of his head, and fucking and slamming into me.

A typhoon of love like this can't last long, and after a few moments, he snarls and buries his face in the side of my neck. I think he bites me, but I'm so far out of it, and so full of sublime ecstasy myself, that I can't quantify a different kind of feeling.

All I register is joy, and the pulse and leap of his cock inside my body.

We lie there, sort of thrown over the low wall together, in a heap of thunderstruck sensation, for what must be several minutes. My nipples are pulsating and bottom feels like it's been roasted, but I don't care. I love the throbbing heat and the sensation of Sebastian's belly and his rumpled clothing shoved haphazardly against the site of his handiwork.

"That was sensational, love," he whispers, recovering first as he almost but not quite always does. I feel his mouth on my neck again, gently kissing this time, not biting, "You're a wonder." He's still inside me, albeit soft, and it's as if he doesn't want to part us. His hand is on my bare belly, fingers spread, just holding us together.

"I love you," I whisper. The words seem most apposite. Always true, and applicable in any situation where my husband is concerned.

We linger like that, murmuring sweet nothings, Sebastian adorably solicitous after what he did with the switch. He promises gentleness, a relaxing bath with an expensive essence that always soothes in these cases, and decrees that we can fuck with me on top for the rest of the holiday.

This makes us giggle, and giggles start lighting fires again... but just as I feel him hardening inside me once more, there are shouts somewhere down the path, and the sound of tramping footsteps.

In a flash, Sebastian pulls out, hauls up my jeans and panties, and swathes his Belstaff around him. Then, he tugs my own coat closed, and hustles me to the back of the shelter where we plonk ourselves down upon the bench.

I grunt when my sore bum hits the seat. But by the time another couple, the argumentative pair from the room next door to us, stomp along the path, remonstrating loudly with each other, my husband and I are sitting together, primly bundled up in our coats and having a civilized conversation about something we didn't really watch on the television last night.

When the combatants are out of earshot, we both laugh like maniacs, and finally put our clothing fully to rights. I even manage not to cry when the clamps come off.

"Come on, gorgeous," Sebastian urges me as we set off down back to the hotel, but at a stately pace in deference to my sizzling hind parts.

At the foot of the hill, though, he pauses, takes my face

between his two hands and kisses me again, very slowly and reverently.

"You're beautiful," he tells me, "And you know I love you, don't you?" He grins, and his pale blue eyes twinkle. "Especially when you've got roses in your cheeks..."

I twinkle back at him, and return his kiss with equal tenderness, my heart as happy as my bottom is rosy pink.

Add the Delicious Pain Boxed Set to your Goodreads shelf

AN APPOINTMENT WITH HER MASTER

I have an appointment. An appointment with a master. My master. It's real this time. It's really going to happen.

Mary-Anne Green smiled to herself, her grin nervous and her heart in a tizzy as she remembered the very start of her obsession.

It'd all begun when she'd picked up a book in a second-hand market several years ago—a fantasy set in an imaginary realm in olden times, when richly dressed princes had taken their beautiful young brides across their knees and administered old-fashioned discipline across their vulnerable bare bottoms.

It'd been a shock. What the book did to her. The luridly overwrought descriptions of tingling red bottoms and the strange sweetness that came with them had scared her at first. Not the stories themselves, but what they'd done to her. Cries of pain and cries of pleasure had rung in her mind as she'd read, and at the same time her body had roused. At first she'd been horrified by her own reaction and tried to ignore her own flesh, the heavy, needy ache and the wetness. But pretty soon all that had changed and transformed into a sense of elation and relief. At last she knew herself, and since that day, it seemed she'd just been waiting for this one.

From books she'd graduated to magazines, and from magazines to exchanging ideas with people she'd met on message boards and in chat rooms. It had been a delicate foray, not mentioning the pain-pleasure at first, until she'd ascertained as best she could that they were like-minded. But still she'd remained circumspect, she'd stayed guarded. She'd relished every crumb of information she'd discovered about those who spanked and those who were spanked, but she'd always held back from revealing her own experiences, or lack of them. She'd concealed her own goals and remained an enigma.

And then one day, she'd found a new correspondent. He was very special one, someone as enigmatic as she, but also irresistible. By then already a writer of some small notoriety herself in BDSM circles, Mary-Anne had reached out to a fellow author she admired. Not the one who'd written the fairy-tale fantasies of minor royal personages with majestically tanned bottoms, but another writer, someone possessed of a far greater talent.

When she'd first read his books, Mary-Anne had discovered her true home—a dark, seductive world of profound and ritualistic severity. The descriptions of spankings and thrashings had thrilled her, the talk of canings had made her unable to resist touching her sex. Again and again she would read his books, and again and again they gave her pleasure, conjuring up pictures she could place herself within. Scenarios, inner visions, where it was her bottom beneath the strap or the hand. Night after night, day after day, she imagined herself bare bottomed across the great man's lap, with all her intimate secrets exposed. She imagined waiting, almost in a state of near-climax, for his strong hand to fall, and when it did, she dreamed that she loved the pain with all the fervor with which she might come to love the man. She asked him if he'd send her a photograph, and when he did, it was his inscrutable, pale, seemingly fathomless eyes that looked down on her in her dreams as she lay at his mercy.

As their correspondence opened up and grew more explicit and wide-ranging, it was inevitable that she'd be driven to try to flirt with him. To hint, however obliquely, that for him alone, she could really bare her all. That for his sake she could suffer a real beating and that his blows would be welcome on her flesh. She could hardly believe what she was doing as she typed the provocative words, and she couldn't believe that they were real, even after she'd pressed Send.

Of course, the great man called her bluff, seeing straight through her hints and allusions to her yearning heart. His reply was confident and knowing, yet beneath it, she read a yearning that matched her own.

You could come to me, and I could make it real for you.

The words were simple, yet so seductive she was lost. Without committing herself at first, without a single word to her Svengali, she was already set on the road that led toward him.

Telling herself it was all crazy, she still experimented in order to prepare herself. She stole a ruler from work, an old thing, quite heavy and sturdily made. When she swished it down fiercely on her inner thigh, the pain was sharp but fleeting, and afterward came a sweet, rosy glow. The heat of it bloomed in her skin, yet spread out instantly to her pussy, so close. It sizzled as if *he'd* smacked her, as if *he'd* exalted her to a new level of perception. Insanely pleased with herself and more aroused than ever, she masturbated furiously, embroidering her fantasy and ready for more, much more. So much more.

The next stage, in fact.

In a bold maneuver that turned her on as much as the experimental spanking itself, she sent the man a ruler that was the same as the one she'd used on her own thigh. It was accepted with a magnificent, amused arrogance that thrilled her, the perfect answer to her call, exactly what she'd wanted. He described what he would do to her, what she would do to him, and specified the logistics of their meeting. Reading his response, she was a teenager in love again, but this time in love with the right man. With him, it wasn't weird to be submissive and obedient to his whim; it made her powerful and right-feeling, not an oddity. Lying in her bathroom, on her back, swishing her bottom with her own sturdy wooden ruler, she imagined herself miles and miles away, lying on her front, across his knee and trembling before him. Or, in an exciting variation, he might put her across the back of some beautiful antique chair and thrash her buttocks with whatever implement he chose.

All the dreams in her mind made her smile, something she did more and more these days. She grinned to herself because within her fantasy, he did all these things because *she* willed it as much as he did.

But what anguish might the pain, the real pain, cause her? What would the stinging, the smarting, the pure fire scorching her untried bottom, do to her? Would the *real* thing be way beyond her fancies?

And now, oh God, the momentous day was here.

Dressed carefully, according to his exhaustive instructions, Mary-Anne made her way toward his house. She'd been amazed to discover that he actually lived quite close to her. Had she met him or seen him on a street or in a shop and never known it was him? What did it mean for her that he lived so near? Did it mean... did it mean there was a future if today went as well as she hoped?

Riding in a taxi, she kept her face straight—amused, yet keeping it inside. Nobody would have thought her sexy today to look at her, but she felt like a goddess, high above them all. Beneath her sober skirt were the exquisitely beautiful black lace panties her master would be expecting to see; although, after the thoughts she'd been having for the whole of the journey, certain areas of them weren't nearly as pristine as they'd been when she'd started out. She'd been sticky wet almost before she'd been out of her door.

Arriving at the posh address he'd given her, she reached out with a shaking hand for the doorbell. Its tuneful ringing announced a point of no return, and for a microsecond it scared her. What if it was all a disaster? What if *he* wasn't up to the job, not what she'd wanted or hoped for? What if the subtext of need and yearning she'd sensed in his letters —that so accurately matched her own feelings—was an illusion? It wasn't too late to turn and run for her life, but just as she dithered, the door opened.

There stood her master, just as tall and lean and distinguished as he'd appeared in his photo, but far more handsome in the living, breathing flesh—a wealthy bohemian with dark, wavy hair and a twinkle in his eye. Her heart went "bingo" as he took her shaking hand in his, which felt so hard and so strong. She could already imagine its power on her bottom.

"Mary-Anne, at last. How wonderful to finally meet you. Do come in."

His smile was a wonder, and of course she knew him. He was a minor local celebrity, a famous and respected scholar, an author in his everyday life, over and above his secret identity. He was slender and elegant and she wanted to laugh, to shout with joy at the prospect of being punished by such a beautiful man. He was single too, a widower, unattached.

All this ran through her mind as he conducted her courteously into his home, his manner gentle, yet alight with expectation.

"Would you like a cup of tea first? Or a glass of wine?" He touched her on the arm, guiding her forward, and her body thrilled. "Or perhaps a moment to yourself? To... to 'freshen up,' as they say, after your journey?"

The first she declined; the second, she accepted, yes, please, but in a moment; the third she accepted with gratitude. A moment was essential, to gather her scattered wits.

In his old-fashioned, rose-potpourri-scented bathroom, she quaked with a delicious swirling trepidation, almost triumph. Pulling down her panties to answer nature's call—how mortifying if the urge interrupted them later—she discovered a truth she'd been pretty much sure of. Her knickers were damp with anticipation.

What would her master think of her? She knew his real name now, but the title still felt right in her mind. Would he be amused by her uncontrollable horniness? Repelled? Disgusted? She didn't think so.... In fact, she was absolutely certain he'd be pleased—more than pleased.

Returning to his exquisitely furnished study, she nervously accepted her wine. It was wonderful, absolutely luscious, but she was too nervous to really appreciate its finesse.

"Look, do you think we could start? Sorry to sound so impatient... it's just... well..."

"So eager," he murmured, his enigmatic eyes sparkling.

Mary-Anne's heart skipped. He was already in his role.

"You'd better kneel down now, Mary-Anne. And pay attention. I'm going to tell you now what's going to happen to you and about the things that I'm going to do to your bottom."

It took all Mary-Anne's strength not to fall down, much less kneel. The way he said "bottom" was so stern, yet so deliciously sexy. He made the single word sound like a poem.

Slowly, meticulously, he outlined the "bill of fare." First it would be long, heavy spanking with his hand, and then he'd administer certain other punishments of his own choice, ones which he'd decide on as the session progressed. Her buttocks would be punished to a state of perfect, painful, simmering redness—and only then would satisfaction be provided. But he didn't say if it would hers or his own.

"On your feet again now. Raise your skirt," he ordered softly, and with a suppressed gasp, Mary-Anne obeyed him.

Now was the moment to reveal the pretty panties for his perusal, and also the seamed stockings and a narrow lace suspender belt.

"Very nice," he said, steepling his long, narrow fingers and touching their tips to the center of his sculpted lower lip. "Very pretty... Now, slip your panties down to your knees."

It was exactly the command she'd expected, but hearing it made her shake and get wetter than ever. This was no longer a fantasy, a supposition, a story written by either one of them; it was real and the pain would soon come. Her face flushing, she grasped her skirt with one hand and used the other to lower her underwear. Mortified with embarrassment, she parted her slim legs so the knickers—perceptibly fragrant with her feminine aroma—would remain caught around her knees and not fall.

"Come to me," her master quietly ordered, and then he smiled as her discomfiture increased.

It was very difficult to move with poise and grace when your panties had to be prevented from falling. Hobbled and feeling inelegant, she scuttled toward him, her face now bright red.

"Very good," he said, his pale eyes glinting, and then in a movement that was completely unexpected, he passed his narrow hand between her legs. "You're very wet," he teased, "and that's so naughty. This regimen hasn't come a moment too soon."

Unable to help herself, Mary-Anne moaned. The touch of her master upon her, even one so fleeting and casual, had almost precipitated her climax. She felt her intimate flesh quiver and her silky fluid seeped out in a helpless flow.

"Come along, let's have you across my knee," he continued, his velvety baritone magisterial and businesslike. "That bottom needs the weight of my hand." As he spoke, he reached around her and squeezed it, and Mary-Anne gasped as her arousal grew stronger.

Still feeling graceless and clumsy, she arranged herself across his strong thighs. Moving his legs slightly, he adjusted her position and made her bottom rear up perfectly before him. Mary-Anne closed her eyes in an ecstasy of shame, then whimpered as he began to examine her.

Clever, clever fingers traced the curves of her cheeks, then dipped into the deep cleft between them. She cried out as shrill as a little girl when his touch lingered against her tiny rosy portal, and then she shook and kicked as his finger patted and teased her there.

"Tut-tut," he said sternly as he circled and tantalized.

"Don't you realize this bottom is no longer your own property? That it's mine to play with and to do with as I will?"

Sobbing her apologies, she felt her sex surge and ripple, roused to pleasure by the profoundly rude play.

"Now, my dear, to business. Let's proceed with the task that you're here for." His voice was low and crisp, and a second later his hand was fiercely hard.

Mary-Anne had never expected this much force from just a simple bare palm, and she squealed out in her pain and pure shock.

"Ah yes, my dear, it smarts, doesn't it?" he observed in amusement as that hard hand rained down a fearsome volley. The spanks seemed to come faster than a human arm could deliver them and covered her whole bottom with an uncanny precision.

Smack! Smack! Smack! The impacts continued remorselessly, covering her bottom cheeks with a glowing veil of pink. She could feel her skin tenderizing and becoming incredibly hot as the wetness between her legs gently flowed. Cupping one cheek in his fingers, her mentor stretched her open and then laid a series of smart spanks across her anus.

More excited than ever, Mary-Anne cried and cried, tears of confusion, and wonder, and yes, pain. It hurt like hell, but she didn't even try to escape him. It was his will to spank her thus, his will to seek out the most sensitive and intimate parts of her bottom and turn them to flaming soreness with hot blows.

His will, but also hers equally. A befuddling miracle, but exactly what she'd craved for a long, long time.

When her bottom was a steady, throbbing scarlet, her master paused for a moment in his task. Once again, he began a close examination, pressing and squeezing at the redness he'd created and letting his fingertips rove freely in her cleft.

"So wet," she heard him murmur, and one digit bored inside her. "It's unseemly that a girl could flow so much."

His words were absurd. He called her a girl, but he wasn't even all that much older than she. It was simply a strategy, and a fulfillment of all they'd discussed in correspondence. She'd played the role in her letters of a naughty, confused neophyte, which was true in a lot of ways. She'd expressed faux horror at getting aroused over the thought of pain, of her bottom being bared and punished, and he'd promised to teach her a lesson about "real" punishment. The fact that her sex was wet and swollen was a sign of sweet success in their mutual endeavor, not a wrongdoing in need of further discipline.

"Clearly, a hand-spanking goes nowhere in taming you," he said. His severity was feigned too, but it still made her tremble. "We must now progress to harsher measures."

Tipping her off his lap, he instructed her to stand in the corner with her skirt raised and her panties still around her knees. Mary-Anne was aware that her crimson bottom would be on show to anyone who came into the room now and almost longed for her master to have a guest. She imagined herself standing there for quite a considerable period while tea was served to a number of interested visitors. She heard imaginary conversations, unknown people discussing the condition of her bottom: its shape, and its redness, and its suitability for various canes and whips. She almost felt inquisitive observers reaching out to finger her fieriness and test the firm resilience of her cheeks. Some might even slip a finger into her sex.

She was almost swooning as her master came across to her.

"Still nice and hot?" His voice was like silk as he tested her flaming bottom cheeks with an ungentle hand. "Answer me, please, Mary-Anne," he commanded, pulling her this way and that and then massaging her cleft, slowly and wickedly.

"Yes... Yes, sir, I'm still v...very hot," she faltered, gulping furiously as he slid a hand round and caressed her at the front too, fingertips working in a pattern.

"Then it's time to make you even hotter," he said, whisking away the delicious, pleasuring touch. "Come with me, and we'll see what we can do."

Still hampered by the knickers dangling around her knees and flooded by the tantalizing shame of it, Mary-Anne followed her master out of the room and up a flight of stairs. At the top, he urged her to shuffle along a corridor and around a couple of corners, and then he conducted her into a sober, mahogany-paneled room. It was another elegant bookroom in reality, but in her imagination, and possibly his, it was a dungeon. She imagined them surrounded by punishment implements of every kind, hung from racks and from pegs, fearsome but imaginary.

The only real dungeon fixture was a small but sturdily made oak trestle that stood in the center of the room. The crosspiece was thickly upholstered and covered with soft red velvet, and each upright had a restraint at its base.

Had he purchased it or had it made especially for her?

"Now, Mary-Anne, I want you to take off all your clothes, then drape your beautiful white body across that bar, as elegantly as you can."

Slowly, Mary-Anne obeyed him, taking every care to move as gracefully as she could. It wasn't easy. Her nerves made her tremble, and, aware of his preferences, she retained her panties around her knees as she removed her other things. She even kept them in place as she removed her stockings, unhooking her suspenders and holding the knickers at half-mast as she tugged her hose down her legs from beneath them. The last item she dispensed with was her suspender belt, spreading her thighs to retain her panties as she unhooked it.

"That's charming, my dear," said her master, sounding pleased, and if she wasn't mistaken, impressed. Keeping her smile to herself, she felt just as pleased herself. "So much so that I think you may keep your little panties."

Mary-Anne tried not to breathe hard. Her tangled knickers made her feel even more naked, even more "presented" and subjugated. They were a symbol of her loss of free will and to be in that state made her sex ache and get wetter than ever.

"And you may wear these too." He held out some objects he'd retrieved from the sideboard while she was busy undressing: a thin, black velvet choker and a pair of very high-heeled, black patent leather shoes.

Knowing she must look foolish in her hobble, Mary-Anne fastened on the choker and then stepped into the high stiletto heels.

In them she swayed and almost fell. She had no grace and no power; she was at the mercy of her own sense of balance. Nor could she set her feet apart and brace herself—with her panties around her knees she was next to helpless.

"Come along, Mary-Anne," her master urged gently. "I'm waiting... Don't you want to obey me?"

Befuddled by the gorgeous shame, she couldn't speak a word, but just nodded and began to totter forward. When she felt his hand on her arm, guiding her, she almost wept with emotion. She'd wanted to manage alone... and yet in another way, failing was exquisite.

Melting with weakness, yet completely enraptured, she let her master arrange her across the bar. His movements were neat and methodical, almost impersonal, and in moments she was cuffed and secured. Her belly was pressed tightly against the red velvet upholstery and each wrist was buckled firmly to an upright. At first she was surprised that her legs were left unfettered, but then she realized that her panties confined her as effectively as a set of manacles, forcing her to part her thighs to a precise, revealing distance so the black lace garment slipped no further than her knees.

Mary-Anne felt fearful and defenseless, yet drenched in a strange sense of peace. There was nothing she could do, nothing she had to do, and nothing she wanted to do. Her master had relieved her of all responsibility and the heavy weight of choice. Life was very simple, very clear to her now; there was no decision to make—she only had to submit, and hurt.

And hurt she would.

"I will punish you now, with this," her master said calmly, holding the familiar ruler in front of her blurring eyes. It was different now, somehow: heavier, gleaming as if he'd polished it, strangely innocuous, yet almost sentient with menace. "It will be extremely painful, and you may cry out if you wish to. In fact, I encourage it... But I will not stop until I've administered six hard strokes." He paused then, his cool hand delicately brushing her shoulder, then her throat, and then her jaw as he raised her blushing face so he could see it. "And after that... Well, we'll have to see what happens afterward, won't we?"

With that, he stepped away from her, behind her, and made ready. Mary-Anne could hear the sibilant swish of the thick ruler as he tested its flight through the air, and its passage seemed to cut her fear in two. She felt ready, accepting, perfectly willing, her peacefulness so deep that it glowed in her heart as a radiant light.

She'd never felt happier in her life. Never before had she been so perfectly in the right place and with the right person.

Then the first blow fell and she screamed; the sound of her voice was high and thin.

"One," her master intoned solemnly while her bottom blazed along a wide, blinding line. White lights danced behind Mary-Anne's closed eyes, and she could hear a voice —hers—keening and whining like banshee or a mad thing. She tried to quiet down, but her mouth wouldn't obey.

"Two." The pain came again, like a cable laid across her, shooting six hundred thousand volts through each soft cheek.

"No! No! No!" she whimpered.

Then she heard "Three" as the next stroke whistled down.

The pain was deeper each time: more solid, more biting, more intense. Four and five seemed to merge into one mass, and when six came, she no longer had breath to scream, but whispered, "Master... oh, Master... oh, Master..." as her bottom leapt and danced, her lower limbs no longer under her control.

The agony in her flesh didn't seem to diminish as the moments passed; it simply seemed to alter in its quality. From bright, piercing brilliance, it damped down to a heavy, pounding throb. As it wound through her senses, Mary-Anne found her perceptions sharpened and intensified. She could smell her master's fresh, lemony cologne through the pungency of her own scents, and beneath she detected the faint odor of his sweat. On the highly polished floor, she could see a shadow moving slowly yet revealingly—a dark silhouette that seemed to merge and blend with hers. She heard sounds, crystal-clear sounds: heavy male breathing, a sliding zip, a tiny gasp.

Finally and wonderfully, strong hands clasped her bottom, and as the torture flared, she welcomed its flaming kiss. She was lifted, adjusted, and painfully maneuvered. Her panties were ripped—yes, ripped—from around her thighs, and then something hard, imperious, and latex-clad probed her pussy.

I love you, Mary-Anne's mind whispered as her melting body opened. She smiled in an ecstasy of joy as he forged into her, thick and imposing, shoving hard in rough thrusts. His animal enthusiasm was completely at odds with the controlled elegance of all his actions thus far, and even though every time he pushed in, he hurt her striped bottom cruelly, his desperation granted power and equal pleasure to her too.

His wild, blasphemous shouts exalted her spirit. When she gripped him with her pussy, that made him sob. And redouble his efforts.

It was a wild ride, an agonizing gallop, and her ascension to bliss.

When he reached beneath her and touched her clitoris, she matched his profanity... then came like an avalanche, praising his name, his real name, sharing his climax.

Later, Mary-Anne lay in his bed, facedown, almost floating. Her bottom still throbbed ferociously, and she knew it was striated with six substantial and overlapping red lines, stark and vivid. But she'd never been happier in her life, and the weight of her master's hand—Benedict's hand—resting lightly at the small of her back was like an angel's touch, a blessing on her suffering.

"You're magnificent.... You know that, don't you? Everything I ever dreamed."

He was lying beside her, also on his front, with his face turned to hers. He was as exhausted as she, and she was in no doubt he was equally as happy. There was no way a man could fake that telltale glow.

Gentle now, he'd been stringent earlier, freeing her from the trestle, half carrying her here and plowing her again and again, on her back, on this bed. His hammering her against the mattress had been like beating her buttocks all over again, but she'd relished it, out-and-out invited it, dragging his hands to her punished flesh and compelling him to clasp her stripes as he pounded into her, gasping incoherently.

Locked in a combat of pleasure, they'd climaxed together, time after time, until exhaustion claimed them.

"You were pretty fabulous yourself, considering," she murmured, shifting her pelvis against the mattress, aroused once more despite feeling wrung out and barely half awake. "I would never ever have known your secret.... You were perfect."

"Yes, I wasn't bad, was I?" There was a smile in his voice as the tip of his finger brushed the very end of one of her stripes, making her hiss. "In fact, I think I was pretty damned outstanding for a 'master' who's never mastered anyone in real life ever before."

"You were perfect. Everything I ever dreamed of too." Her heart fluttered. It was more than the pain. More than the pleasure. Everything they'd shared in their long, deep, no-holds-barred correspondence had been completely fulfilled in their meeting in the flesh. Fulfilled and exceeded beyond her wildest hopes and fantasies, both her erotic ones and her gentler dreams, born of emotion.

"So, we're both perfect..." His voice was thoughtful, as measured as his tantalizing hand. "In which case, wouldn't it be a shame not to... to continue? And progress?"

He was still her master, but the little hesitation made him her equal too. It only confirmed he too wanted more than just the sex.

It made her able to say, "Yes, that's what I want too. And I think we should collaborate... write together. We've made fantasy into reality between us, so now we can make reality back into fantasy."

He laughed, softly and happily. "I thought you'd never ask."

Slowly, slowly, he ran a fingernail down the fiercest of her stripes, making her moan and hiss through her teeth, while at the same time he slid his other hand beneath her belly, working into her fleece and finding her clit with perfect accuracy.

Scratch and circle, scratch and circle, scratch and circle; within seconds she was coming hard, yet again.

"Shall we make a story of this too?" he purred in her ear, even as she climaxed.

"Yes... Oh God, yes, please!"

While Mary-Anne groaned and laughed, all a-jumble in her pleasure, Benedict's answer was a happy sigh, a breath of triumph.

"I love you," he whispered, still fondling her sticky sex.

Discover Mary-Anne and Benedict's next sensual adventure in Another Appointment

NAUGHTY THOUGHTS

"Are you having those naughty thoughts again, you bad girl? I can always tell, because your eyes start to cross."

Terrence accompanies his accusation with a swirl of his hips, a move that nearly blows the top of my head off. It also nearly dislodges said naughty thoughts he's accusing me of. But not quite. They're so naughty I can't seem to shake them, despite another virtuoso hip-swirl that makes me groan and claw his back.

"Back with us again, are we?" he gasps, laughing as he shags. He really is the most fabulous, fabulous lover.

"Yes! Yes!" It's half gasp, half cry, all genuine. I don't have to do a Meg Ryan when I'm with Terrence. He's just gorgeous and he knows how to do the business. And if that wasn't enough, he looks like a movie star too. And not one of those mindless action hunks, mind you, all pecs and teeth and tan. No, he's like the more thoughtful kind of star, one with lots of grey cells and a major league sense of humor to go with his exceptional body.

And he's on top of me now, going like a jackhammer.

Or he was.

For a moment, he raises himself up on his elbows and looks down on me. His handsome face is sweaty and a little flushed, but that only makes him sexier than ever. And even hotter for the look in his eyes. They're narrowed, sort of cute but sly, and shiver-inducingly knowing. He gives a little shake of his head as if he's read my mind. I hope he has, and I hope he likes what's in there.

He gives me a soft little kiss, on the corner of my mouth. "Maybe I should go down on you again for a while. That'll stop you wool-gathering while I'm giving you my fanciest moves, you naughty bitch." He licks his lips and that makes him look incredibly wicked.

You could spank me.

I open my mouth. I almost say it. But I don't. Not yet. That's a delicious treat I'm saving to surprise him. Doesn't stop me thinking about it, though.

"I like your moves. I love them!"

He tilts his head, and a comma of thick brown hair dangles in his eyes. "I should bloody well think so, woman." He smoothes my hair out of my eyes too, and wipes the sweat from my brow. "You'd better brace yourself, because there's more of the same incoming."

"Do your worst!" I growl, and he swirls again. "Or preferably, your best!"

I have to close my eyes now, because they're crossing from the pleasure of him this time, and either way, I must look like an idiot. Hitching around beneath him, I find an even better angle, if that's possible, and with another small kiss, then a bigger one, he starts to swing in and out again, with all the smooth power of a human reciprocating engine. Supporting himself on one arm, he strokes my body at the same time, his fingers as clever as his gorgeous erection is potent.

I start to rise higher, straining against him, arching, reaching, savoring.

And the naughty thoughts return to sweeten climb.

In my mind, in a heartbeat, we're in a dark, dangerous room somewhere together. Is it a dungeon? Why, yes, it is… Here are the dingy, encrusted walls, the flickering torches in their sconces, the chains. And here's Terrence, but not quite the man who's currently making love to me. Well, he's the same, and just as sumptuous, but a darker version, more dangerous and exotic.

In bed, I grab at him, excitement building, my fluttering sex roused anew by my kinky, yummy notions. "Baby," he growls, sensing every subtle and not-so-subtle response.

In my imaginary subterranean prison, he prowls around me, a slightly smiling figure all done up like the dream of a master. He's stripped to the waist, clad only in form-fitting leather jeans and knee-high boots—apart from a platinum-studded collar round his neck. His thick brown hair is slicked back with water or gel or pomade, and his bare chest gleams in the torchlight as if he's oiled.

"Well, well, slave," he purrs in the mirror world.

Me, I'm strung up, my wrists in cuffs that dangle on chains from the smoky ceiling. I'm all done up like the dream of a slave, my body trussed in a corset of tight-laced satin, my feet in high-heeled pumps, a gag in my mouth.

A shudder runs through me in each parallel world as he tweaks my nipple and makes me squirm.

Oh god, he's so beautiful when he's stern. The mouth that kisses so softly is sculpted and cruel, and his warm brown eyes are black with power and lust.

As he slaps my bottom with the flat of his hand, I start to come. And come in the real world too, in bed, lying underneath him. Straining for the best, the finest, the highest orgasm, I arch against Terrence, my heels dragging against the backs of his calves, my fingers flexing like talons, gripping his bottom.

I scream as I soar to heaven, while his phantom self smacks my naked flesh, again and again.

Afterwards, we lie against the pillows, both slumped and sweaty, breathing hard. Multiple orgasms have knocked the stuffing out of me, and even Terrence, with all his prodigious sexual stamina, looks momentarily shattered.

"What the hell were you thinking, Vickie?" He turns to me, and I see he's sharper and more with it than I imagined. Those clever brown eyes of his gleam with knowledge, almost as if he really were the master of my fantasy. "There was something dirty and devious going on that turned you into a wildcat, wasn't there?" He does that sinful lip-licking thing again. "Come on, woman, tell the truth or you'll regret it." His mouth curves into a deliciously evil smile, and I'm back in heaven.

Oh, the threats... oh, please bring them on!

Suddenly I'm not tired at all. Now's the time to tell him. Because I've a sneaky feeling he probably knows already. He's got this uncanny knack of reading me, and it turns me on.

I prevaricate, gnawing my lip. An act, obviously.

"Vickie?" he prompts. There's a hint of sternness there, and for a vertiginous second, I can't tell whether it's real or fabricated. My pussy flickers again despite my previous surfeit of pleasure.

"I... um... well, it was just a little fantasy I sometimes have." Little? Who am I kidding? It's big and it's bad and it's beautiful. "I... I don't mean that our lovemaking isn't satisfying... it's just I have these thoughts sometimes." Lots of the time, and I'm dying to share them. "I can't help myself, but it's not you, it's me. I... You're a fabulous lover."

His eyes are on me. Steady and strangely bright. Knowing again. The devil, he's teasing me. He's read my mind as easily as if my eyes were made of glass. Suddenly he is the man in the dungeon and twice as dangerous.

"But not quite fabulous enough," he growls, pursing his lips, fighting that sunny, sexy "let's get it on" smile of his. "Spit it out. What do you want? What dark and depraved perversion do you think about when you're already having bloody good sex start with?"

I would point out to him that he has a very high opinion of himself, but now's not the moment. Especially as I hold that high opinion also.

"Well, you see... it's like this. I sort of like men to spank me. It's a 'thing' of mine, you know?"

His eyes widen. He chews his lip. He looks perplexed. Oh, give the man an Oscar! But he can't disguise the merriment in his eyes.

"Good lord, you are a wicked little pervert, aren't you?"

"But I do like ordinary shagging too, honest! I just that like I spanking as well."

"I see." He's killing himself here. I swear he's dying to burst out laughing.

"Perhaps I'd better go." Throwing myself into my penitent role, I start to slide out of bed, ready to feign a search for my scattered clothes.

But he stops me with a firm hand on my wrist. "Oh no you don't! I think we need to get to the bottom of this." He has to turn away then, and I can see his broad shoulders shaking. "I'm going to get a bottle of wine. And then we'll discuss it properly. No messing about."

Then he strides naked across the room, stalking towards the door, his gorgeous cock swinging. It's a bit perky again. More than perky.

Oh God, I can't wait!

A few minutes later, after I've rushed to the bathroom and tidied my hair and everything, I sneak back into the bedroom and he's already returned.

But he's not in bed. Chin resting on his steepled fingers, he's sitting in the armchair, dressed again. Well, sort of. He's wearing his black jeans, but his chest and his feet are still bare. Whether by accident or design, he's managed to make himself even more magnificent than ever. He's the man of my dreams, literally and figuratively, and covering up his gorgeous goods only makes me feel more vulnerable by contrast.

"So, spanking, eh? There's a thing," he says, his voice level. He takes a measured sip of red wine from the glass that he's set on the bedside table at his elbow, and staring at me, his smooth brow crinkles in a little manufactured frown.

I feel awkward. Unsure of myself. This is all so real, all so sudden. Do I get back into bed? Or just sit on the edge of it? I feel off balance, standing here naked while he's sitting, clothed, calmly drinking his wine.

He doesn't seem to have poured a glass for me.

"Yes... sorry... it's just a kink of mine. I can't help it."

His fine eyes narrow. Is he cross? Because I haven't shared this with him sooner? I start to feel shakier than ever, even though my pussy is already swimming.

"I never said there was anything wrong with it."

I'm starting to feel more and more disorientated, but in

a good way. When I begin to edge towards the bed, he makes a little quirk of his lips that's so perfect it almost stops my heart. So I hover, feeling giddy, out of my depth.

He draws in a deep breath, sets aside his glass, and stretches. "So, I suppose we could try a bit of this spanking. Give it a whirl."

My heart thuds madly. I feel a new rush of hot honey between my legs. If he really is what I suddenly suspect he is, I've hit the mother lode here.

He's Mister Perfectamundo. Everything I've ever wanted and a whole lot more.

"So, how does it go? What do you usually do?" He clasps his hands loosely in front of him, his head tipped slightly on one side, the glow from the lamp shining on his sleek, dark hair.

"All sorts of things. Sometimes the man spanks me over his knee. Sometimes I lie across the bed, on my face, and he punishes me."

"What with? His hand? Or something else?"

We really are getting in deep here. Sliding through layers and layers. My heart flutters like a bat on crack. "Yes, sometimes his hand. Sometimes something like a belt, or even a leather slipper. Sometimes, um, toys."

"Toys?"

"Something like spanking paddle... or a ruler... or even a riding crop."

Now, for some reason, I find it hard to look at him. His gaze is like a laser, sweeping over me.

"Fascinating." He pauses, a long slow beat. "But how do you want to start? What do you think is the best way to begin?"

My eyes are cast down. I stare at the carpet. But in my mind I can see his strong legs, his experienced thighs spread just the precisely right amount. His lap—with a growing bulge beneath the dark denim of his jeans. He's become his mirror-self from my dungeon fantasy.

I drag in a breath with all the effort I would have to exert if the atmosphere had turned to water, or to gel. "I... I think I'd like you to spank me across your knee, if that's all right?"

"Yes, I think that would be okay." His voice is neutral, serene, soft. And yet humming with subliminal power. "But isn't there some kind of ceremony, a form of words at least? Don't you think it would be a good idea, maybe, to call me 'master' or something?"

That thud in my heart picks up speed. I feel as if I'm in the middle of a vortex. "Y...yes, master."

"Well, let's get started, shall we?"

Eyes still down, I pad across to him, and he offers a hand to help me go over his lap, and assume the age-old position. His thighs feel firm and solid beneath the rough denim, his feet perfectly planted, everything in balance. As I lie there, I feel safe. He won't let me fall.

He adjusts his position slightly, and I adjust mine, and his hand settles on the small of my back to steady me.

"You have a beautiful bottom, slave," he purrs quietly, with just a microsecond of artistic hesitation. That warm hand of his brushes my bare cheeks, first one, then the other. And again, stroking lightly, burning hot. I suppress a pathetic mewl when one finger traverses the length of my bottom crease.

"So, these men who spank you... Do they just play at it, or do they really spank you hard?"

"Yes. Sometimes. Quite hard." The words are difficult to get out. I can barely breathe.

"And do you like that?" He touches my anus and I

squeak. Which he seems to ignore as a regrettable aberration.

"Yes! No! Sort of!" I can't see his face, but my imagination presents me with him smiling. Supreme. A happy god, playing with me in ways other than physical. But when he speaks, he still imbues his voice with that thread of theatrical doubt.

"Well, I'll have to see what I can do then. Wouldn't want to disappoint you after all this hard, serious spanking you've had in the past."

I open my mouth to protest that it isn't all that much, but then, out of the blue, his first smack lands and it just takes my words away.

It's not a heavy slap, but not light either. It hurts. And it isn't by luck or blind intuition it's landed right on the crown of one bottom cheek. He knows exactly what he's doing and has done all along.

"That's amazing," he says, sounding strangely awestruck.

That *is* amazing, I think, just struck.

He's hit me in the perfect place and with the perfect weight. Like Pavlov's dog, my body responds. My pussy ripples in anticipation of more, more, more, and my lubrication starts to seep down onto his jeans. Unable to control myself, I wriggle and rub myself against him.

"Are you supposed to do that?" His voice is mildly questioning, but there's nothing unsure about the way his fingertips trace the hot hand-shaped mark they've just created. And there's nothing tentative about the way he slaps me again, on the other cheek this time.

I squeal, already out of control in a way I've never been before. But of course, I've never been with a master this experienced.

How on earth has it taken me this long to realize that fact?

"I'll bet you're not supposed to do that, either," he remarks, sounding joyful, as if he's really enjoying getting into the swing of things. His arm certainly is, because he's slapping steadily now. If I had brain cells left over to ponder such matters, I'd wonder what on earth I've done to deserve this bounty, a man with a perfect natural gift for corporal punishment and a beautifully honed skill. But I have very little brain power available at the moment, nothing left over from the writhing, the whimpering, and the blatant and desperate way I massage my crotch against his hard thigh beneath dark denim.

He smacks and smacks. I squirrel around and sob. And what happens eventually is almost inevitable, I suppose.

It all gets too much for me, and hitching myself up a bit, I sneak a hand beneath myself and slither fingers into my pussy. While he's still spanking me, I find my clitoris and rub it feverishly.

After that I'm a lost cause, and within seconds, I climax hard. Very hard. Almost too hard. I jackknife on his knee, almost falling off, but he holds me tight. My pleasure soars as his fingers press my tender redness.

I fall back into my body again as a sniveling, glowing, still pulsing, incredibly happy mess. As I half slide and half fall in a guided fashion to the carpet at his feet, he reaches into his pocket and then hands me a handkerchief.

"You've done that a hundred times before, you sly brute, haven't you?" I accuse him from my lowly position as my brain clicks back into operating mode and I start to grin. "All that BS about making me tell you what my fantasies are... You've known all along. You could read the signs, couldn't you? Why didn't you tell me you were into exactly the same thing as me?"

He cups my face, makes me look up at him. His eyes are radiant with knowledge and mischief and power, utterly entrancing—although there's a base part of me that's more interested in his enormous erection and is dying to check that out.

"I suppose I should say sorry for stringing you along," he says softly, the stroke of his finger beneath my chin an elegant counterpoint to the throb, throb, throb in my bottom and in my pussy. "But a master doesn't usually apologize, does he?"

The "M" word makes the pulsation between my legs deeper, hotter—even though it's barely minutes since I came. "No, but you still could have told me," I persist, wondering and hoping that if I provoke him enough he might do more, more, more.

"Indeed... Indeed I could." His beautiful eyes glitter with excitement, danger, desire, and dominance, holding me utterly still as he goes on to remind me of the party where we met and how he sought me out. I'd wondered why he—this peach of a man—had selected me when there were much, much sexier girls on the prowl. I'm pretty enough, but I know I'm a quiet bloomer.

"You're right. I could—I can—read you. I could tell you shared my interests... It's patently obvious from the way you carry yourself." I shudder at the thought of me beaming out those secret signals, an open book to a *cognoscento* like Terrence. "So I decided to see how long it would take for you to admit it."

"Oh, for heaven's sake! You devious bastard!"

"Tut, tut... Naughty, naughty," he chides, but the look in his eyes makes me wetter and warmer than ever. "Why so cross? It's what you wanted, isn't it? Part of the game? The dance?"

I want maintain to my mega-defiance act, play at being aggrieved, but the greater part of me, the truer part of me is thrilled, light-headed. He is my ideal, and I can't believe my luck.

"Um... yes... I suppose," I answer with a last mulish flicker.

"Finally, she admits it. I should punish you for being so obstinate, shouldn't I?"

My heart lurches. Can my steaming bottom take it? So soon? When I'm so red, so sore? But my sex lurches too, gathering itself and readying. I almost come without a touch at the thought of more.

"Yes, master," I whisper, lowering my head in acknowledgement and starting to shuffle into position in order to get up and across his knee again.

"Oh no, Vickie... not that. Well, not right at the moment." He adjusts his own position now, conveying an eloquent message and gilding it with a gentle but still delightfully devilish smile.

Oh yummy, I think, reaching out to unfasten his zip.

THANK YOU!

Many thanks for reading **Delicious Pain**. I do hope you enjoyed the wickedly sexy games of these four passionate couples and the loving forever relationships that each duo share.

If you'd like to be notified when my next book or story is up for release, please visit **portiadacosta.com** and sign up for my mailing list, for news, previews and reader competitions. And if you'd like to discuss this title with other readers, search for **Portia's Reader Lounge** at Facebook and join up for relaxed chat and probably a few giggles!

You can also follow me on Twitter **@PortiaDaCosta**. I love to have a natter with readers!

Reviews are a wonderful way to help other readers find books, so please do consider reviewing **Delicious Pain** at Amazon, Goodreads, or your favourite site of choice. I appreciate all reviews I receive.

"Another Appointment" (Mary-Anne and Benedict's

second story) is available now in my "His by Choice" series as an ebook at Amazon, iBooks and Kobo.

I also have another series with kinky romance elements called "Secret Pleasures". "His Secret", "Their Secret" and "Her Secret" are available in ebook, with "Her Lover's Secret" to follow.

I also write erotic romance in a variety of other flavours and you'll find a selected list following my bio.

ABOUT PORTIA

Portia Da Costa is a *SUNDAY TIMES* bestselling British author of romance, erotic romance, and erotica, whose short stories and novels have been published in the UK and elsewhere since 1991. She loves creating stories about sexy, likeable people in steamy, scandalous situations and has written for various publishers over the years, including Black Lace, HQN, Spice Briefs, Samhain Publishing, Carina Press, and a good many others. Though her best-known titles are mainly contemporary erotic romance, she also enjoys writing super-hot Victorian historical romance, and erotic paranormals. She's even turned her hand to a bit of erotic sci-fi and horror on occasion.

Recently, her Black Lace contemporary erotic romance *IN TOO DEEP*, reached Number Five in the *Sunday Times* paperback fiction chart, with only books by E L James and Sylvia Day outselling her!

When Portia isn't writing she's usually to be found loafing around, watching the television or reading the works of Agatha Christie, Sir Arthur Conan Doyle or Stephen King. Sometimes all three at once, which can be confusing. She lives in the heart of West Yorkshire in the UK, with her long suffering husband and their four beloved cats: brother and sister Mork and Mindy, curmudgeonly but lovable Felix, and Monsieur Le Prince, a rescue cat from France.

Find out more about Portia at the following...

Twitter: **http://twitter.com/PortiaDaCosta**
Website: **http://www.portiadacosta.com**
Blog: **http://wendyportia.blogspot.com**

Portia is also on Facebook and chats in **Portia's Reader Lounge**

SELF-PUBLISHED EBOOKS BY PORTIA

A Pretty Weird Bloke
An Appointment with Her Master
Another Appointment
Daring Interludes
Delicious Pain (boxed set)
Delicious Pleasure (boxed set)
Fire and Ice
Forbidden Treasures
Glint
Her Secret (Secret Pleasures #3)
Her Lover's Secret (Secret Pleasures #4)
His Private Dancer
His Secret (Secret Pleasures #1)
In Sebastian's Hands
Lessons and Lovers
Object of Desire
Naughty Thoughts
Power of Three (In Love with Two Men #1)
Tempted by Two (In Love with Two Men #2)

The Efficiency Expert
Their Secret (Secret Pleasures #2)
Wesley and the Love Zombies
Wild in the Country

MAINSTREAM EROTIC ROMANCE BY PORTIA

The Accidental Trilogy
The Accidental Call Girl
The Accidental Mistress
The Accidental Bride

Black Lace Contemporaries
The Gift
The Red Collection
The Stranger
In Too Deep
Entertaining Mr Stone
The Devil Inside
Suite Seventeen

The Ladies' Sewing Circle (Victorian setting)
In The Flesh
Diamonds in the Rough
A Gentlewoman's Quartet

Three Colors Sexy
Discipline of the Blue Book
Ritual of the Red Chair
Ecstasy in the White Room

ANOTHER APPOINTMENT - EXCERPT

Mary-Anne and her master, Benedict, have been together for a while now, but they never stop exploring new BDSM fantasies and games together. Although she's happily his by choice, Mary-Anne is growing in strength and self-confidence in their relationship, and even though she adores submitting to Benedict in their erotic scenarios, as a couple they're very much equal partners.

Their latest wild adventure, devised by Mary-Anne, tests her limits and his inventiveness to the utmost. Is it a step too far, or the gateway to another level of intense sensation and erotic pleasure-pain? And perhaps an entirely new game altogether?

Excerpt:
When she was ushered into her master's study, it was empty. A small fire burned in the hearth, and there were comfy armchairs to sit down in as well as the vast, imposing desk and an equally august leather chair behind it. The slave would have loved to warm herself before the hearth or

relax in one of the chairs, as much as she could with a reddened bottom. But she knew she wasn't allowed to...

Temptation was intense, but she could almost imagine he might have deviously installed a CCTV camera in here so he could keep tabs on her while she awaited his arrival. The longer she stood, the more driven she was to transgress. He was definitely keeping her waiting on purpose. She stood for a full fifteen minutes, feeling unsettled, off-balance, yet more and more and more turned on. Reduced to a mere object, an ornament to decorate the room, she felt her sex moisten anew with anticipation.

The sound of the door opening made her flinch. "Take off your coat, please," said her master matter-of-factly, strolling to his desk and taking his throne-like seat. He was dressed for the country in expensive vintage tweeds, an exciting contrast to his modern, youthful looks.

But it was the intensity in his eyes that made her feel faint. They were pale, level, and very stern. He seemed unmoved when she shed her coat and stood half-naked before him, but she sensed he *was* moved. And that in the depths of those serene eyes, hungry fires burned, far back. Heat and more...

"I should like you to walk around the room a little," he instructed, picking up a pen from his desk and toying with it, turning it end over end between deft fingers.

The slave did exactly as she was told, acutely conscious of her naked bottom and her shaven sex. The perilously high heels made her mince a bit as she walked, and the flesh of her rounded buttocks jiggled. She knew full well that her fresh lash marks would be plainly visible.

"Why were you late for our appointment?" inquired her master as she passed before him for perhaps the tenth time. "You know how I value punctuality."

"I... I...," the slave stammered. The words wouldn't form. Raw desire froze them in her throat.

"Tell me," her master insisted, his low voice silky. "I want details. I want to know everything. All your excuses."

The slave managed at last to speak. Slowly, haltingly, she described the whole sequence of events to him, even her imagined *amour* on the train, which had no bearing at all on her late arrival but was still as important to him as events that had really happened.

"Stand still now," he said as she finished her description of how the chauffeur had used her in the clearing. "Here." He indicated a place beside his desk. "Lean over, please, and press your body across the desk."

Once again, the slave complied without demur, draping herself across the cluttered surface of the desk and feeling documents and paper clips adhere to her belly. With no warning and a delicious lack of his usual finesse, her master began an exploration of her sex.

Printed in Great Britain
by Amazon